Cursed with a poor sense of direction and a propensity to read, **Annie Claydon** spent much of her childhood lost in books. A degree in English Literature followed by a career in computing didn't lead directly to her perfect job—writing romance for Mills & Boon—but she has no regrets in taking the scenic route. She lives in London: a city where getting lost can be a joy.

WINNING THE SURGEON'S HEART

ANNIE CLAYDON

MILLS & BOON

Published in Great Britain 2020
by Mills & Boon, an imprint of HarperCollins*Publishers*
1 London Bridge Street, London, SE1 9GF

© 2020 Annie Claydon

ISBN: 978-0-263-08718-5

CHAPTER ONE

SILENCE FELL. FROM the thirty people who had entered the challenge, there could only be two winners, and it looked as if the judges were ready to announce who they were.

Hannah's friend, Sophie, was bent forward, clutching her knees and stretching the muscles in her back. The most challenging task in a long and challenging day had been saved until last, an obstacle course that had drained everyone. But they'd done it together. Hannah laid her hand on Sophie's shoulder and she looked up, grinning.

'I think you're in with a chance. Not so sure about me.'

'We'll find out soon enough. Are you okay?'

Sophie nodded, straightening. 'We'll all be aching tomorrow.'

This was more than just a matter of winning for herself. Hannah and Sophie had worked together for five years, crewing an ambulance that worked out of Hamblewell Hospital. When the hospital had entered Arial TV's *Hospital Challenge*, lured by a generous cash prize, they'd decided to enter together. The selection day had involved both physical and mental challenges, and was designed to whittle thirty entrants down to two, who would go on to represent the hospital in the televised challenge. Hannah had set her heart on winning with Sophie.

She caught Sophie's hand, squeezing it. A stage had been erected on the open space behind the hospital building, and in the heat of a summer's day there was almost a carnival atmosphere amongst the spectators. The chairman of the judging panel had picked up the microphone and was tapping it to see whether it was working. A frustrated murmur travelled through the crowd that had come to watch and cheer the competitors on.

'Get on with it, mate.' Sophie whispered, and Hannah nodded. The suspense was getting to her as well.

'The judges have come to a decision—'

The microphone cut out suddenly, and Hannah rolled her eyes. If they'd wanted to keep everyone on tenterhooks for as long as possible, this couldn't have been planned any better.

There was a short pause as the microphone was inspected and pronounced fit for use, without the need for any further tapping. The judge smiled, turning once more towards the crowd.

'Sorry about that... As you all know, today's winners will go forward to represent Hamblewell Hospital in the Hertfordshire heats of *Hospital Challenge*, the first of which will be hosted here next Saturday. We hope you'll all be here to cheer our team on. We've been obliged to choose just two winners today and our task hasn't been easy...'

There was a pause. Everyone was holding their breath already, and if the guy didn't get on with it, someone was going to pass out. It was just as well that there were plenty of medical staff on hand...

'Hannah Greene!'

Hannah heard a cheer go up, somewhere far away. She felt Sophie grab her, hugging her tight. Suddenly it felt as if her legs weren't going to carry her.

'Go... Go.' Sophie had freed her now, and was pushing her towards the stage, where the judges were all on their feet and joining in with the applause.

'Sophie...' Hannah didn't want to go alone. She'd

thought that both names would be announced together, and taking this walk without her friend seemed impossible.

'You've won, Hannah. You've got to go and shake the man's hand.' Sophie gave her one last push, and a path opened up in front of her through the other competitors. She walked towards the podium in a daze.

Then it hit her. Sophie was going to be next, it was impossible that the judges hadn't seen the way they'd encouraged each other in completing the challenges. They were already a team, used to going together into every kind of situation. Hannah climbed the steps onto the stage, shook the judges' hands and then turned to the crowd, throwing her arms up. Everyone cheered wildly, and she could see Sophie jumping up and down, suddenly finding that last bit of energy.

'We've obviously made a popular choice.' The judge smiled, waiting for the cheering to die down, and there was silence again. 'And going on to join Hannah for *Hospital Challenge* is Matt Lawson…'

What?

Hannah tried to smile, but it felt as if her own achievement had suddenly turned to dust. She didn't even *know* Matt Lawson. She looked for Sophie, and she was cheering along with everyone else, seeming not to notice that it was her name that should have been called.

The crowd parted, and a man began to walk towards the stage, stopping to shake a few hands as he went. Hannah *did* know him, although not by name. He had a reputation as being an excellent surgeon, but many of the female staff ignored that and concentrated on his looks. Hannah herself had been guilty of a little objectification on that score…

His sun-coloured hair and the tan gave him the look of someone who spent more time outdoors than inside. Probably blue eyes. Hannah had imagined the blue eyes and then consigned the whole image to the *look-don't-touch* category.

She felt herself blush as he shook the judges' hands, and then grinned at her. Blue. They were blue, the shade more intoxicating than she'd imagined. Dark, like a Mediterranean sea.

That was where he belonged. On a holiday she had no intention of taking. Not here, not in her real life. He congratulated her, and then turned to wave to the crowd. This was *not* happening.

She stood, trying to smile, for what seemed like an age, until they were allowed to climb down from the stage. Sophie was the first to get to Hannah and hug her.

'I'm so excited… And you've got the dreamboat as a partner!'

Hannah felt tears of exhaustion and disappointment in her eyes. 'I don't want him. Why didn't they pick you?'

Sophie puffed out a breath. Hannah was about to get one of her friend's reality checks.

'Look, I'm not going to pretend that I'm not disappointed. But you did a lot better than me, and so did he. Did you see the way he got over that climbing wall?'

Yes. Hannah had looked, just as Sophie had. Matt Lawson had been in the second group around the obstacle course, and they'd both seen the way he'd negotiated the steep wall. And she'd dared to notice that he looked just as good—better actually—in action than he did when she'd seen him walking along the corridors of the hospital.

'I can't do it on my own, Sophie. We're a team.'

'Well, you're just going to have to get used to being in a new team, aren't you? I'll be cheering you on all the way.'

'But…' This sounded a lot like self-pity. She should be thinking about how Sophie must be feeling, not having been chosen after all the effort they'd put in. 'I'm so sorry…'

'Nonsense. We said that we'd be happy if just one of us was chosen, didn't we? This is *my* achievement as well, we did it together. Give me a break, will you?'

They'd said it would be enough if just one of them won. Hannah hadn't actually meant it. But Sophie was glowing with joy, and it would be unfair if she didn't feel it too.

'You'll stick with me, won't you? I can't do this without you.'

'Are you kidding? I'll be with you all the way. You'll be there for both of us, eh?'

Matt hadn't seriously expected to win this thing. As the only member of the surgical team who'd had any chance of being able to negotiate a climbing wall, he'd been strong-armed into signing up for the challenge by his colleagues, who had all been keen to have someone represent them. He'd stepped up his gym routine a bit for the last three weeks, and that had been about it.

He'd seen Hannah and her partner, making their way around the obstacle course. They were both fit, and both up for the challenge, but Hannah was clearly the stronger of the two. Although the tasks they'd encountered today were meant to be done individually, he'd seen Hannah slow a little once or twice, waiting for her partner to follow so that they could pace each other around the course.

They were a team. They wore matching T-shirts, emblazoned with the logo of the ambulance service. He knew that the nature of their job meant that they had to rely on each other, and that the ambulance crews had a fierce sense of pride. He wondered how Hannah felt about being teamed up with a complete stranger.

She'd seemed less than enthused about the judges' decision when he'd been called up to the stage. But as she walked towards him across the grass, she was smiling. Matt had to admit that it was a very nice smile, at that.

'Congratulations.'

'That was a surprise…' He felt strangely at a loss for words. 'For me, I mean. You were a dead cert to win.'

She blushed a little. It was a fine accompaniment to

her smile. 'You made it over the climbing wall in one go.
I took two.'

Matt was privately of the opinion that she could have
done it in one. His automatic assessment of her mobility
and strength told him that the wall shouldn't have been a
problem for her and that her partner was the one who'd
taken two goes. The judges had clearly seen that as well,
and Matt decided not to mention it.

'I'm looking forward to the next round.'

Hannah nodded. 'Me too. Would you like to meet up?
To train?'

That sounded rather more enticing than Matt had supposed it might. Hannah's was the kind of beauty that was
enhanced by the application of a little grime and sweat.
This morning, he'd noticed her chestnut hair tied back in
a shining plait at the back of her head. And, of course, her
smile. But as the day had gone on, he'd started to appreciate her fearlessness and tenacity. She was messy and exhausted, but she still shone.

'I'm afraid I can't this week, I have a pretty full schedule
at work. I imagine they're going to be throwing the unex-
pected at us next Saturday, so I guess the best we can do
is just keep up the fitness training and get a good night's
sleep on Friday.'

That obviously wasn't the answer that Hannah was looking for. It was too bad, because he couldn't just put off a
few operations because it happened to suit him. She should
understand that.

'Okay. Well... I'll keep training with Sophie. As long as
you don't mind.' She motioned towards her partner, who
was walking towards them.

'Why should I? If it works, don't mess with it.'

She and Sophie had the kind of partnership that Matt
had observed in others, and had never really experienced
for himself. He was part of a team at work, in just the
same way that she was, but he confined that to knowing

the strengths and weaknesses of his colleagues and what they could reasonably be called on to do during working hours. Hannah and Sophie were obviously friends, and he almost envied it.

'Hi. I'm Sophie. Congratulations. You did a great job and you really deserved to win.' Sophie held out her hand and Matt took it. Her manner was a little more open than Hannah's and her grin a little easier, but somehow it didn't reach into the corners of his soul the way that Hannah's did. But then no one had any business with his soul, that was his to contend with.

'Thanks. You and Hannah are a great team…'

Sophie threw her arm around Hannah's shoulder, laughing. 'I think I've hit my limit today. You and Hannah can go on and win this thing.'

That was obviously important to both of them. Matt hadn't really thought much about it, he'd reckoned on giving a reasonable account of himself and then going home. But suddenly he wanted to be a winner. And he wanted Hannah at his side, winning with him.

'The hospital could do with the money.'

'We're all relying on you two.' Sophie laughed. 'No pressure, obviously.'

'Pressure? What's pressure?' Hannah murmured the words quietly.

Sophie chuckled, nudging her friend in the ribs. 'Don't listen to her, Matt. Hannah's very focussed at times.'

He could see that already. And he liked Sophie immediately, she was the kind of woman that he usually chose to spend his free time with. Conventionally pretty, with blonde hair and blue eyes, she seemed easygoing and uncomplicated. Hannah, on the other hand…

Hannah was compelling. Beautiful. Almost certainly not the right kind of woman to get involved with, because bonds made with Hannah might not be easy to break. Matt dismissed the idea. No one was going to get involved with anyone, he should relax and look at this as an extension of his work. Money for the hospital *was* an extension of his work.

'We'd better get going...' Hannah was scanning the crowd intently, obviously looking for someone. 'I'll see you next Saturday, then?'

A whole week suddenly seemed a very long time to wait. But Matt hadn't planned on winning today, and he was going to have to fit his training sessions in whenever the opportunity presented itself.

'You know where to find me if you want me?'

Hannah nodded quietly, and it was Sophie who answered. 'Yes, we know. We'll leave a message with the surgical unit...'

Matt watched as the two women walked away from him. Sophie was obviously reliving one or other of the obstacles, tracing shapes in the air in front of her to illustrate the point. Hannah was listening intently. He wondered if she ever gave herself a break and loosened up a bit.

'Mum...!'

A small boy, of about six, was running across the grass towards them, followed by an older woman. Even if he hadn't called to her, Matt would have guessed this was Hannah's son, his tawny eyes and red-brown hair matched hers almost exactly. Hannah stretched out her arms in an expression of joy, falling to her knees, as the boy ran straight into her arms.

If she'd employed half the exuberance that she'd shown just now, she would have floated over the obstacle course, instead of battling her way through it. Sophie and the older woman were chatting and laughing together, and Hannah was doing a little victory dance with her son. The thought that he wanted to do a very different kind of victory dance with her was enticing and entirely inappropriate, but it was the kind of image that was difficult to erase from his memory.

It would fade. Memories *did* fade when you were a stranger, always on the move. Matt had learned to travel light, making no lasting personal attachments to hold him back.

He'd been travelling light since he was eight years old. Always running, always trying to leave behind the bad memories. But they were the ones that had caught up with him now, crowding in and obscuring the sun. As clear as if it had all happened yesterday, and blocking the view of Hannah and her family.

Matt had known that his father had an uncertain temper and that he'd sometimes hurt his mother and made her cry, but he knew now that his mother had protected him from the worst of it, locking him in his bedroom or sending him to a friend's house to spend the night. Afterwards he'd seen his mother wince in pain as she'd bent or reached for something. There had never been any bruises on her face, but as he'd got older Matt had begun to understand that was the one place his father had never hit his mother.

His father had hurt him once. Just once, but Matt still remembered the pain and the terror of being unable to escape the hand clamped firmly around his arm. Now he thought of it as a good thing, because it had been the final straw that had made his mother pack their bags and leave.

At first it had been exciting, a taste of the kind of freedom that Matt hadn't even realised existed. They'd changed their names, using his mother's surname instead of his father's, and had embarked on a new life, in a new town. And then his father had found them and they'd run again. Another new life in another new town. Matt had forgotten how many there had been. In the end he hadn't bothered to make new friends, because he'd known that he and his mother would be moving on again soon.

Matt watched as Hannah played with her son in the late afternoon sunshine. They seemed happy, carefree. No looking over their shoulders…

Until Hannah *did* look over her shoulder, straight at him, and caught him staring. Matt raised his hand, giving a smile, and she returned the gesture. Then he turned and walked away. He had no business wanting Hannah's warmth. He needed her as a teammate, and that was just for the next few weeks. After that, he'd be moving on again.

CHAPTER TWO

LIGHTS, NO SIRENS. There was no lack of urgency in getting their patient to the hospital, but Hannah needed to be able to hear his laboured breathing. And Sophie needed to be able to hear if Hannah called out to her to stop.

The ambulance swayed a little as it turned into the hospital. Sophie specialised in giving their patients a smooth ride, but speed was of the essence. She'd radioed through to the hospital, asking for immediate assistance, then put her foot down.

They drew up outside A and E, and Hannah concentrated on monitoring their patient, a middle-aged man who'd been hit by a bus. Sophie climbed down from the driver's seat, opening the back doors of the ambulance, and Hannah saw a tall figure in surgical scrubs waiting outside.

'What are you doing here?' As usual, Sophie voiced the question that was on Hannah's mind. Matt Lawson should be in the operating theatre, not A and E.

'Just helping out.' Matt was smiling and relaxed, but when Sophie and Hannah manoeuvred the stretcher out of the ambulance he moved quickly, his eyes on their patient as he guided them through the melee of people in A and E to an empty cubicle. It wasn't unusual for the doctors in A and E to place a call for specialist help from other departments when they were busy, and Matt must have been the one to answer.

Matt had clearly been told about her provisional diagnosis, and everything necessary to confirm it was laid out ready. He pulled on a pair of gloves, listening as she relayed Ben's name and what she'd already observed about his condition. Taken together, his symptoms indicated that Ben might be in the early stages of a tension pneumothorax, and if it went unchecked the progressive build-up of air in his pleural cavity could prove fatal.

'I'll need you to help me lift him. I appear to be flying solo.' Matt murmured the words to Hannah quietly, so that Ben couldn't hear.

'I'll stay. Sophie and I are on our lunch break now.' It looked as if everyone was busy with other patients, and Matt would need her help.

'Thank you.'

The warmth in his smile prompted an inappropriate thrill in Hannah's chest as her heart beat a little faster. She pulled on a disposable apron and gloves, trying not to think about how Matt's assessment of her actions seemed suddenly all-important.

They lifted Ben onto the bed, and Sophie folded the ambulance stretcher, ready to take it back out to the vehicle. Matt was talking to Ben as he quickly examined him, and Hannah readied the ultrasound machine, handing the probe to Matt as soon as he turned around to look for it.

'Great, thanks.' Even that small approbation meant more than it should. Matt was studying the screen on the ultrasound carefully, his brow furrowing for a split second before he made his decision. 'You were right, this is a tension pneumothorax. I'm going to do a thoracostomy—can you assist?'

Hannah nodded. Ben was conscious and Matt had undoubtedly left out the word *emergency* in describing the thoracostomy for his benefit. But they had no time to lose now. Hannah had taken Ben's shirt off in the ambulance, and now she raised his arm, smiling at him as she placed it behind his head.

'What's…happening…?' Ben began to move restively. Breathlessness and agitation were two of the symptoms that Hannah had already noted.

'The doctor's going to do a small procedure that'll help you to breathe more easily. We need to you stay as still as you can.' Hannah tried to reassure Ben and hold him still without getting in Matt's way. She'd never before felt so conscious of the touch of another body, working next to her.

Ben flinched as Matt swabbed the area at the side of his chest, moving again so that he could see what Matt was doing. Hannah couldn't blame him, but he had to keep still.

'Ben, this will be over soon. I'm going to inject an anaesthetic now. Look at Hannah, not me.'

Matt's voice was relaxed and calm. The kind of voice that you needed to hear when you were afraid and in pain. Ben quietened, his gaze fixed on Hannah, and she gave him a reassuring smile.

'Very still now.' She heard Matt's voice behind her and leaned forward, preparing for the inevitable reaction when the needle went into Ben's chest. Matt was working quickly and deftly, but no amount of skill could render the procedure painless.

Ben groaned, gripping her hand tightly, and Hannah heard a tell-tale hiss of air as the tension in the pleural cavity was relieved. Matt withdrew the needle carefully, taping a plastic cannula in place.

'All done. You did really well.' Matt smiled at Ben as he started to examine him again, to check that the procedure had relieved his symptoms. 'Hannah and I are a team, you know. We're entering a competition to win money for the hospital.'

This wasn't just idle talk. Matt was assessing Ben's ability to understand and reply.

'Yeah? You're lucky to have her.' Ben's face was less ashen now.

'Don't I know it.' Matt smiled, and tingles ran down Hannah's spine. She reminded herself that Matt's sudden impulse to chat was for Ben's benefit, not hers. 'I'm rather hoping that she'll keep me in line.'

Keeping Matt in line felt like a delicious and yet difficult prospect. Hannah shot a smile in Ben's direction. 'It looks as if I'm going to have my work cut out for me.'

'Just let me know if he gives you any trouble.' Ben's hand found hers again and Hannah gave it a squeeze. 'I'll sort him out for you.'

'Thanks. I might take you up on that.'

Matt chuckled, and his glance of approval told Hannah that he'd seen exactly what she had. Ben was much less breathless now, and he was more alert. As Matt set about checking Ben's blood pressure, one of the A and E doctors arrived with a nurse, ready to take over from them.

Matt briefed the doctor, while Hannah said goodbye to Ben. When she left the cubicle, she saw that Matt was already at the far end of the busy space outside but he'd stopped by the door and was waiting for her. Hannah stripped off her apron and gloves, and went to join him.

'Spotting the early signs of a tension pneumothorax isn't easy in the best of circumstances, let alone in the back of an ambulance.'

Hannah nodded. Matt's easygoing humour had given her no clues about what he thought about the course of action she'd taken, but she was pleased that he approved.

'We were close to the hospital, and the symptoms were inconclusive. Doing a thoracostomy in the back of an ambulance isn't ideal, and I decided it was better to keep going so that Ben's condition could be properly confirmed...' She bit her lip. Matt's gaze was making her feel very nervous.

'You don't need me to tell you that you made the right decision, do you?'

'No, I don't.' She really wanted him to, but that had more to do with his blue eyes and his smile than it did with any medical considerations.

Those eyes, and the thought of how it had felt working next to him, were playing havoc with her senses. And Ben wasn't here to concentrate her mind on other things. Suddenly it felt as if she was standing too close to Matt, but stepping back now was only going to betray her embarrassment.

'I should be getting along now. Sophie's probably waiting for me, with some lunch.'

Matt nodded amiably. 'I'll see you on Saturday.'

'Yes. Saturday.' Hannah tried to think of something friendly and encouraging to say, and came up empty.

As he walked away, she couldn't resist watching him, telling herself that assessing the width of his shoulders was something to do with deciding on Matt's ability to handle whatever they were confronted with on Saturday. She jumped, as Sophie seemed to appear out of nowhere and caught her staring.

'I'd say you don't have too much to worry about on the teamwork front.'

Hannah shrugged. 'It's different. We both knew what had to be done…'

'Yeah. Keep telling yourself that. You two looked as if you were reading each other's minds.' Sophie grinned at her. 'Come on. Let's take our break while we can. I could murder a cup of tea.'

Hannah nodded. There was a lot to do before Saturday rolled around, and she could begin to feel nervous about that later.

The four teams had started to gather on the open space behind the hospital building at seven thirty, for the first of four Saturdays that were intended to single out one team to represent Hertfordshire in the finals of *Hospital Chal-*

lenge. Many of Hannah's friends and workmates were there to watch, and the other teams had brought carloads of their own supporters.

Hannah had been issued with three red T-shirts, with the name of her hospital emblazoned on the back, and she was wearing one. The other teams were wearing blue, green and yellow, so that they could be picked out easily by the cameras. There was a large marquee that no one was allowed access to, and everyone was eyeing it with a mixture of curiosity and apprehension.

Matt was nowhere to be seen. Hannah had greeted the other teams, shaking hands with them and keeping her eye out for the splash of red that she hoped might announce his arrival.

Finally she saw him. Strolling across the grass towards her, wearing the same red T-shirt, with a pair of cargo pants and trainers. They hadn't been told what to expect, other than that anything might be thrown at them today, and Hannah had made the same decision.

'Hello.' She wanted to ask where the hell he'd been, but that might not be the best start to this new partnership.

'Hi. Sorry I'm late.' He looked at his watch. Matt wasn't late, it was just that everyone else had been half an hour early. 'I stopped by my office...'

'Doing *real* work, then.' Hannah tried to smile.

Matt shrugged. 'This feels surprisingly real at the moment.'

One hint that he wasn't as laid-back about all of this as he made out. 'I'm a bit nervous, too.'

He laughed suddenly. 'Did you get the pep talk from Human Resources?'

'The one about how everyone's going to be watching, and the good name of the hospital is on our shoulders? And how much the hospital can do with the cash prize, if we win?' Hannah quirked her lips down. 'Yes, I got it.'

'And of course we both feel a great deal better after

that.' There was a twinkle in his eye, and Hannah felt herself relax.

'So much better. Nothing like the weight of expectation to give us wings. I wonder what the other teams have up their sleeves.'

He nodded, motioning quietly away from the groups of people that surrounded them. Hannah followed him to a quiet spot in the shadow of the hospital building.

'My office window is just up there.'

Hannah followed the line of his finger. The windows of the second-floor surgical suite looked out over the people milling around the marquee. It occurred to her that Matt hadn't been up there, working.

'What have you seen?'

'I reckoned that the first thing we needed to do was assess the competition. We're not the only team who don't know each other all that well. Look at the blues and the greens.'

Hannah looked. The two green T-shirts were giving each other a high five, which she'd seen them do before, and it was obviously for the benefit of the people around them.

'I'd agree with you about the greens. Too demonstrative.'

He nodded. 'And the blues have their backs to each other most of the time.'

'The yellows seem pretty tight.'

'Yes, they are, I know them. Jack and Laura crew an ambulance, working out of Cravenhurst Hospital.'

Matt looked suddenly uncomfortable. Hannah had tried to hide her feelings but he must know that she'd wanted to be partnered with Sophie.

'So we reckon that two of the other teams are like us, and don't know each other too well. But the yellows are already very used to working together...' Matt's brow puckered in thought. 'Maybe we just pretend we have a tension pneumothorax to contend with. We did pretty well there.'

Looking beyond the personal, and functioning as a team.

A self-contained unit, relying on each other and seamlessly compensating for each other's weaknesses. That was so easy to do with Sophie, and so very challenging with Matt. Relying too much on him seemed like stepping into a vortex, which would claw her down into the kind of relationship that she'd promised herself she'd never have with a man again.

So don't look at him as if he's a man. He's a person, a fellow competitor.

As soon as the idea occurred to her, Hannah dismissed it as ridiculous. Matt was all man, and every nerve ending was urging her to be all woman in response.

'Perhaps for a start we should tell each other our greatest weakness.' Hannah puffed out a breath. You couldn't just ask that of someone without being willing to go first. 'I'll start—'

He shook his head, laying his hand on her arm, and suddenly her greatest weakness wasn't her tendency to plan everything down to the smallest detail. Her greatest weakness was Matt's touch…

'Why don't you tell me what *my* greatest weakness is? When you find it. In return, I'll tell you yours.'

That was a great deal more challenging. But this was supposed to be a challenge after all.

'Okay. That could work.'

'And in the meantime, concentrate on our strengths. We'll need those if we're going to win.' He gave her a gorgeous smile. 'And we *are* going to win, aren't we?'

'Yes, we are. Do you want a high five?' Hannah had just seen the greens do it again, and this time it seemed a little less confident than it had before.

'Is that your thing?' He turned his gaze on her, and she shivered as the vortex seemed to beckon her once more.

'No, not really.'

'Right, then. Let's disappoint Human Resources and dispense with that.'

She liked his quiet humour. The way he looked for real answers, and didn't just follow what everyone else did.

Then she saw it, glistening in his eyes. Despite all of his outward unconcern, Matt wanted to win too. He wanted to make them into a team that could win together. She'd been too quick to jump to conclusions about him.

'How long do you suppose we'll have to wait?' There was obvious activity going on amongst the production crew, but no one seemed very interested in rounding up the contestants yet.

Matt chuckled. 'Probably until our nerves are just hovering around fever pitch.'

He didn't seem to be anywhere near fever pitch at the moment. If Hannah hadn't known better it would have infuriated her, but Matt was obviously working things through in his own way. Maybe they'd just taken the first step in their team-building exercise.

Matt was used to waiting. The quiet, measured activity of the operating theatre, where lives hung in the balance and the slightest slip could make a world of difference to a patient, had taught him that being ready wasn't a matter of straining at the leash.

The competitors had been called to a roped-off area to one side of the tent, but it didn't look as if anything else was going to happen any time soon. Matt sat down on one of the benches that had been provided and Hannah sat next to him, fidgeting. He could almost feel the tension radiating out of her.

'The little boy you were with last week. He's your son?' Maybe talking would calm her a little.

'Yes.' She smiled suddenly, that wide open, joyful smile that he'd seen last week. 'His name's Sam.'

'How old is he?'

'Six.'

That got the basics over. 'Where is he today? With his father?'

Hannah's smile slid from her face. That clearly hadn't been the right thing to say, and Matt wondered why on earth he'd made the assumption. He should have just come out and asked if Hannah had a partner, if he'd wanted to know so much.

'No, with my mum. She's going to bring him along here later to hear the results announced. It's just me and Sam. His father isn't on the scene.'

'I'm sorry… I didn't mean to pry.'

'That's all right.' Mischief kindled suddenly in her eyes. 'If we're going to be a team we should get to know each other.'

Matt laughed. 'Okay. Matthew Robin Lawson. Thirty-six years old, born in Newcastle, single. I've been here for a year, and before that I was working in Glasgow.'

'You've moved around a bit?' Matt shot Hannah a questioning look and she smiled. 'You don't have a Newcastle accent.'

'Yeah. The only family I'm in touch with is my mother, and she lives in Devon. I go wherever there's a great job that will challenge me.'

It sounded suddenly as if the life he'd made for himself was missing something. The vital ingredient that Hannah seemed to possess, a family and good friends. But this was what he knew. He'd grown up as an outsider, and that was how he felt comfortable now.

'And you watch people.' It came unerringly out of the blue, and combined with the warmth in Hannah's eyes it carried a momentum that almost knocked him backwards.

'I guess so. We used to move around a lot, and I found it pays to sit and watch for a while when you're the new kid in school.'

She seemed to see more in that then he'd said. It felt good to be accepted, but Matt knew that being accepted wasn't everything. Being safe was everything, and he didn't want Hannah to know about that.

'And you?'

'Ah. Hannah… Do I *have* to tell you my middle name?'

'You do now. How bad can it be?'

She grinned. 'Hannah Eloise Greene.'

'What's wrong with Eloise?' It suited her softer side perfectly.

'It's…well it's a bit girly, isn't it? I'd prefer something a bit more…' She waved her hand, as if she were groping for the right word. 'Adventurous, maybe.'

'Flash? Jet?'

Hannah laughed, and Matt warmed to his theme. 'How about Olympia, if you want to go classical? Or Juno?'

'No! Olympia and Juno are far too elegant for me. And one of my friends called her little boy Jet.'

Matt chuckled. 'Flash it is, then.'

'Okay. Hannah Flash Greene…it's got a ring to it. Twenty-six years old, born right here in this hospital. My father died six years ago, and Sam's father and I split up before he was born. My mum and I bought a house together, and she looks after Sam when I'm at work. I'm lucky, because it's a good arrangement for both of us.'

'I imagine it's great for her to be able to spend time with her grandson.' Matt hadn't had too much contact with his family. Staying below the radar had meant that his mother had considered it unwise to visit either set of grandparents, and his aunts and uncles had been just names to him.

'Yes. She didn't know what to do with herself when Dad died. I was away, and…' Hannah shrugged. There was something she didn't want to say, and Matt didn't intend to press her. This had just been something to talk about, he hadn't meant to share any secrets.

'Contestants! This way, please.' One of the production assistants called out suddenly and they both jumped.

They'd been told that there would be cameras in the tent,

and that they should do their best to ignore them. Inside, there were four sections, each screened off from the others. A smiling woman handed Matt an envelope.

'Everything you need is in here. Follow the red markers.' She gestured towards the canvas door that bore a red flash. 'You can go now.'

Hannah unzipped the doorway, and Matt saw trestle tables, piled high with medical equipment. He watched as another canvas door at the far end of the tent was opened, revealing a carport with a small red car parked in it. They stepped inside and someone zipped the doorway closed behind them. It was an odd feeling, being completely alone with Hannah, but knowing that they were being watched by cameras. He opened the envelope, sorting through its contents.

'Car keys and a map... Phone... Ah. Instructions.' He handed the sheets of paper to Hannah, craning over her shoulder to see.

'Okay...' She scanned the paper quickly. 'We've got to take the things we think we might need, and wait for the phone to ring. The red car's ours, and we'll use it to get to a medical emergency that's happening somewhere inside the red ring on the map. We don't know where yet, or what kind of emergency...'

'Sounds like a normal day for you.' Matt grinned at her, spreading the map out on top of one the boxes that were heaped on the trestles.

Hannah studied the map, frowning. 'The red ring's a good thirty miles from here.'

'Which means we have to make a decision. We can't get everything here into the car, so we either take what we think we'll need and make a start, or we wait here for the phone call and risk being delayed in traffic.'

Hannah nodded, looking up at him. Perhaps she was waiting for him to make the call.

'What do you say, then, Flash? This is your area of expertise, not mine.'

She grinned suddenly. 'I say we go. We can open up the boxes and take just the amount we might need from them.' She pointed at the large box of dressings. 'Even if we need all that, there are only two of us and two people can't apply that many dressings.'

'Agreed. Why don't you make a selection and I'll put everything into the car.'

She raised an eyebrow. 'You're sure about that?'

'Positive. I'm used to having whatever I could possibly need within reach. I'll go with your best guess over mine.'

'All right, Robin...' He raised his eyebrows and Hannah chuckled. 'You asked for that. You can start with the defibrillator and the oxygen kit—we should definitely take those.'

Fifteen minutes' concentrated work, and they were ready to go. Hannah had used plastic bags and torn wrappers to contain reasonable amounts of as many different things as possible, repacking boxes and labelling them with a marker pen. She'd added a couple of large zipped bags to their provisions, commenting that they were obviously there for a reason, and picked up the bag of sandwiches and the six-pack of water bottles, stowing them in the foot-well of the car.

'Can you see what the others are doing?' Matt drove out of the carport, and he caught an enticing trace of her scent as she craned round in the passenger seat, trying to see what was going on behind them.

'Yep. Yellows have gone already. Since they're an ambulance crew I wouldn't be surprised if they haven't done the same as us. Blues and greens look as if they might be staying put.' She twisted back round in her seat, surveying the road in front of them. 'I hope we've done the right thing.'

'We've done it now. We look forward, not back.' Matt could feel a tightening excitement in his chest. This wasn't just about winning, not even just about bringing home the cash prize for their hospital. Suddenly, it was Flash and Robin, on the road together. Ready to face whatever was thrown at them.

CHAPTER THREE

HANNAH HAD PICKED a spot that gave easy access to main roads in all directions, and was approximately at the centre of the circle. They got out of the car, stretching their legs, and even though it was only ten thirty, she broke open one of the packets of sandwiches. Who knew when they'd get a chance to eat later on? After ten minutes, the phone rang. Matt answered it, listening carefully and scribbling notes on the back of the map.

'It's at Lloyd Court. Apparently there's someone who's collapsed. No further details at the moment.'

Hannah rolled her eyes, spinning the crust of her sandwich into a nearby waste bin. 'What, like where he is or what might be wrong with him?'

'I suppose they think that's far too easy. They'll pass further information through to us in the next half-hour. Do you know Lloyd Court?'

She nodded. 'Yes, it's a country park. And it's huge, it'll take us all day to find someone there.'

Matt handed her the car keys. 'We'd better get a start, then.'

As Hannah turned into the wide avenue that led to the heart of the country park, he got another call. He listened carefully and then turned to her.

'Apparently our patient's had a heart attack. There was one phone call from him, he couldn't give his exact location but he said he'd been walking on the estate here for around half an hour, and that he was surrounded by trees. His name's Justin Travers and they've given me a phone number for him, but apparently he's not answering.'

The spike of adrenalin made a clear summer's day move into even sharper focus. 'Why give it to us, then?'

'That's what I'm wondering…' Matt was fiddling with the phone as she drove, and Hannah concentrated on the road ahead, turning into the car park that sprawled to one side of the visitors' centre. She got out of the car, opening the hatchback.

'What are you doing?' She started to unload the boxes, sorting out what they would need for the walk ahead of them.

'Just looking…ah! Got him!'

'What?' Matt didn't seem to appreciate that this was an emergency situation. Okay, so it was a fake emergency situation, but they had to pretend it was real.

'I did an internet search for the number. There's a business connections page for a Justin Travers and he's obviously a walker. Look…' Matt held out the phone and Hannah glanced at it, then went back to unloading the boxes from the car. She grabbed the two rucksacks and started to fill them with the things they might need.

'He's a made-up person, Matt. He's not going to have social media.'

'Or they're testing us. What would you do if you were in this situation for real? You'd try to find out who he was if you could.' He handed her the phone and Hannah scrolled through the page that was displayed. The guy was a self-employed computer consultant, and his hobby was walking. He'd been on a recent expedition to Mount Kilimanjaro, and his contact number was clearly shown. When she scrolled down a little, his other hobby was listed as '*Watching* Hospital Challenge'. That couldn't be a coincidence.

'I was wrong…' She suddenly felt very small. Matt

hadn't underestimated the complexity of the challenge the way she had. He hadn't dismissed her experience either. She hadn't shown him that respect.

He shook his head. 'No, we were both right. We need to get moving now and expand our search area, because someone like this is going to be able to walk further in half an hour than most people could.'

'What do you suggest?'

'Serious walkers tend to travel in a straight line and if that's what he did, then there's just one area of woodland that's approximately two and a half miles from here.' Matt indicated an area to the west.

'And we go there first?' There was woodland to the east as well, but that was only a mile away. Further on was an area of grassland.

'It's a risk. Under normal circumstances there would be search parties out, going in every direction, but we have to choose. We can't split up, the instructions say that we both have to be at the scene together.'

Think. Think!

Hannah turned, staring at the hill that led away to the west. This was the challenge that any experienced walker would set themselves. When she faced Matt again, he was regarding her steadily.

'Okay. I agree, we go west.'

Matt shouldered the heavier of the two bags, and added two bottles of water to its weight. He set off at a fast walk, and Hannah wondered if she should remind him that they needed to pace themselves. He probably was pacing himself. She watched his back, gritting her teeth. It was a matter of pride that she could keep up.

But after a mile her head started to swim, and the muscles in her legs and shoulders were screaming. She stopped, letting her bag fall to the ground. Matt turned.

'Perhaps we should have some water…' Just a few minutes' rest, and she'd be ready to go again. He nodded, handing her one of the water bottles.

He was waiting for her. Matt made a show of consulting the map, but they both knew exactly which way they were going as the woodland at the top of the hill stood starkly on the horizon. One minute. Just one minute and she'd be ready to pick up the bag and go again.

'Drink a little more.' He picked up the half-empty water bottle that she'd put down on the grass, handing it to her. Then he caught the strap of her bag, shouldering it with his.

'No... Matt, I'll be okay...'

'We have to get there together. If I get tired, you can take the bag back.'

His tone was quiet. Gentle, even. Not like the shouted exhortations to keep going that she'd trained with.

'Don't give me permission to give up...'

He grinned suddenly. 'You don't have my permission to do anything other than keep walking. I'm going to need you when we get there, so let's go.' He turned, obviously slowed by the extra weight but still able to keep going.

It was a lot easier without the bag. Hannah caught up with him, walking beside him.

'You don't believe in a little encouragement?'

'What, you mean bullying you until you pick the bag up again and start walking? No, I don't believe in that.' He was suddenly tight-lipped.

'Sometimes a bit of a push is what's needed.'

He nodded. 'Yeah. But don't ask me to do it.'

Matt wasn't wasting any words, and it wasn't just the extra weight he was carrying. This was a line that he didn't cross. His relaxed attitude to everything wasn't a matter of *laissez faire*. It was more like a decision about how he was going to interact with the world.

'I get it. If I need any shouting to get me back on my feet, I'll do it myself.'

'I'd appreciate that.' He gave her one of his sudden

smiles. Those deep blue eyes were enough to drag anyone to their feet, heart pumping faster and legs suddenly strong.

'I'll take my bag back in a little while.'

He nodded. 'All right. I can't make it all the way like this.'

He had his strengths, just as she did. And finding them, using them, was a challenge that was both daunting and delicious.

Matt knew what Hannah had been asking of him. He knew that getting her to her feet wouldn't be a matter of real aggression, and more one of channelling her thoughts and reactions towards one clear aim. But he still couldn't do it.

It had been more than twenty-five years since he'd cowered before his father's wrath. Everything he'd done and said had been calculated to please, because when his father had got angry it had been over the smallest things. This wasn't the same, and pressuring Hannah back to her feet wouldn't have been the same kind of aggression that his father had dispensed so freely, but he still couldn't bring himself to do it. It wasn't who he was. What he'd made himself be.

When she took her bag back, he caught the scent of her sweat. Not stale or pungent, but an exciting sweetness, which spoke to his body on a level that he'd learned to ignore. He should ignore her touch, too. Something about the way that she snatched her hand away from his when he gave her the bag told Matt that she felt something too, and he couldn't help but smile.

'We split up?' They'd reached the edge of the woodland, and Hannah took the map from him, spreading it out on the ground. The trees formed a wide band that stretched out ahead of them.

'I think so. I'll walk along the ridge, there, and you take the path.' Matt chose the more uneven, sloping terrain. Physical effort might take his mind off her auburn hair, glinting in the sunlight, and the way that her sweat-dampened T-shirt didn't hide her curves as well as it had.

'Giving me the easier route again?' For a moment her expression told him that she might well argue with that.

'Don't worry. I reckon there are enough challenges ahead of us to go round.'

Hannah grinned suddenly. 'Probably. Thanks, I could do without climbing to the top of that ridge.'

They walked more slowly now, keeping each other within sight and scanning carefully for any signs of the man they were looking for. Matt caught a glimpse of blue, between the trees on the other side of the ridge, but when he scrambled down towards it, he saw that it was an abandoned plastic carrier bag, fluttering in the breeze.

'Anything…?' He heard Hannah's voice, calling to him.

'No. Nothing.' Matt shouted back, and she started walking again. As the woodland area started to narrow, the ridge wound down to meet the path.

'Where *is* he? Suppose we're wrong, Matt.' She seemed suddenly exhausted from the effort it had taken to get here.

'Suppose we're right?'

Hannah nodded, straightening suddenly. 'We'll walk through to the end of these trees, and then double back for a second look, shall we? When we're sure he's not here, we can think again.'

They walked for another ten minutes and then he saw it. Deep amongst the trees, in a patch of bright sunshine, the body of a man propped up against a tree stump. They forced their way through the undergrowth and Matt felt a bramble tear at his arm, catching at the supple branch before it hit Hannah straight in the face. She ducked ahead of him, jogging towards the man and falling to her knees beside him.

Matt wasn't sure what to expect right now. Surely they weren't supposed to carry out resuscitation procedures on what was presumably a perfectly healthy volunteer? Then the man opened his eyes, grinning up at Hannah.

'Hi, there. You made it, then.' He jerked his thumb behind him. 'Go over there.'

Hannah didn't move. 'Are you all right?'

The man snorted with laughter. 'Yes, of course I am. We try to make everything as authentic as possible, but I draw the line at having a real heart attack.'

She frowned suddenly. 'Have you got some water?'

Matt felt for the water bottle in his bag. They'd both been caught up in the illusion, but Hannah had stepped out of it for a moment and seen a real issue. The man had been sitting in full sunlight, and it was a hot day. His face was already a little red.

'Actually, I could do with some. Looks as if I'll be here for a while.' He took the bottle from Matt. 'Thanks. Now go on, will you? Five minutes in that direction.'

Hannah got to her feet, staring ahead of them. She turned questioningly to Matt and he shrugged. He couldn't see anything either.

They walked downhill through the brush, and he saw something amongst the trees. The shape of an expertly camouflaged tent. They approached it, and Matt ducked around the tent flap, seeing a busy crew and four tables, each bearing one of the team colours. He turned to Hannah, holding the flap aside for her.

'Great.' A young woman approached them, beaming. 'Go over to your table…'

'In a minute.' Hannah's grim determination to get the job in hand completed seemed to have deserted her. 'I'd like to speak to whoever's in charge.'

'You're still being timed.' The young woman frowned.

'Then I'd like to speak to them straight away, please.' She shot an apologetic look at Matt and he nodded. He knew now what was on her mind, and he wasn't about to tell her to forget it and hurry her over to the table.

A man responded to the woman's beckoning hand, and hurried over. 'Is there a problem?'

'Yes, there is. The man lying out there is in direct sunlight, and he's got no water, we gave him some of ours. He's already looking a little red in the face, and I'm hoping he doesn't get sunstroke.'

Matt grinned. Go, Flash.

'Um…' The man scratched his head. 'Did he say he felt ill?'

'No. But prevention's always better than cure, and I was sure you'd want to know.' Hannah shrugged. 'Health and safety, and all that…'

She was being nice about it, but there was a hint of firmness beneath her smile. Matt never had to explain what he wanted, he just made a decision and everyone went with it. Hannah must face this kind of situation every day, and she was clearly practised at getting her own way with the minimum of confrontation and fuss.

'Yes, of course. Thanks for letting me know, I'll get straight on it. If we sit him in the shade a little closer to the path, and make sure he has plenty of water, would that be okay with you?'

'That's fabulous. Thanks.' Hannah flashed him a smile, and turned to make her way across to the red table.

'That's very sportsmanlike of you.' Matt shot her a smile, so that Hannah would be in no doubt that he approved. 'The other teams will be able to see him more easily if he's closer to the path.'

She shot him a querulous look. 'You think I should have done anything different?'

'No. I'm just pleased to see that I have a teammate who *won't* stop at nothing to win.'

Hannah flushed a little, then leaned towards him. 'You just wait and see what I'll do if you don't get over to that table. Right now.'

That was almost an incentive to stay put. Hannah could

do anything she wanted with him, the more up close and personal the better. The sentiment must have shown on his face, because she raised her eyebrows.

'Since you asked so nicely...' Matt turned and walked over to the table.

CHAPTER FOUR

THEY'D SPENT ALMOST an hour going through what they'd brought in their bags, and how they would have treated their patient, with two of the judges. About halfway through, the yellow team had turned up, but there was no sign of the blues or the greens. Finally they were allowed to go, walking with one of the production assistants along a path that led to the perimeter of the park, and then being ferried back to the visitors' centre by car.

Matt got into the red car, feeling his back pull as he did so. He reached for the ignition, and Hannah stopped him.

'Your arm's bleeding.' She reached under her T-shirt and into the pocket of her jeans, pulling out a packet of antiseptic wipes that she must have saved from the medical bag she'd been carrying.

Matt was vaguely aware that thorns had ripped through both the fabric of his T-shirt and his flesh at some point, and that his shoulder was stinging. Now that he looked, he could see a trickle of partly coagulated blood.

'It's okay.'

She gave him the look that she probably saved for any of her patients who proved intractable. Half smiling, half determined.

'Okay, so you want to be a man about it. I won't tell anyone. I find that it's in my own interest to keep you as healthy as possible over the next four weeks, so you'll just have to take a hit for the team.'

The stinging felt a little too close for comfort to the scar on his shoulder, which he kept hidden from everyone. But he did what he imagined everyone else doing in the face of Hannah's charm. He pulled the sleeve of his T-shirt up, gratified to find that if he held it in place the dark red mark wasn't visible.

'Oh. Nasty.' Hannah squinted at the gash on his arm. 'Hold on a minute. Sharp scratch.'

'Ow! That's not a sharp scratch. What did you do?' If he was going to forgo being a man about it, then he may as well go the whole hog.

'You had a thorn still in there.' Hannah held up a vicious-looking spike. 'I think there's another one. That might be a slightly sharper scratch…'

It was. But this time it didn't take Matt so much by surprise, and he kept quiet about it. Hannah wiped the wound carefully, and then applied a plaster from her pocket. 'That should hold it. Although—'

'Give it a good wash when I get back? I've got that part…' Matt pulled the sleeve of his T-shirt back down again.

'Yes, of course. Sorry, force of habit.'

She leaned back in her seat, staring out at the sun-dappled grass in front of them. Suddenly Matt didn't want to start driving again. He was used to knowing people in terms of the way they did their jobs, and it didn't usually occur to him to make small-talk about his colleagues' lives. But Hannah was different.

'You know this place pretty well?'

She nodded. 'Yes. We used to come here on Sunday afternoons when I was little. My dad taught me how to fly a kite here.'

It must be nice to have those memories. To be able to access them whenever you wanted and smile.

'You've never thought of moving away?' He was interested. It was an experience that was so very different from his.

'Not really. After my dad died my mum was just…lost. I was away for a while, and by the time I managed to get back, my dad was already gone. I couldn't leave her again.'

'I'm sorry. That must have been very difficult.'

'It was for Mum.' Hannah shrugged off whatever regrets she had of her own. 'He knew that I was coming back for him, he just couldn't wait.'

A tear trickled down her cheek, and she wiped it away impatiently. Matt wanted very badly to comfort her, but wasn't sure whether she'd accept it.

'I imagine that there isn't much you can tell people that you love that they don't already know.'

She nodded. 'That's what I think as well. I hope so, anyway. My biggest regret is that I never got to tell Dad that he wasn't to worry about Mum, because I'd look after her.'

'I dare say that you know what your son's capable of, even better than he does, at times.' Matt really wasn't qualified to give advice on families. But maybe all that time when he was a kid, spent watching other people's families, studying them carefully from the outside, gave him a slightly different perspective.

Hannah laughed suddenly. 'Yes, you've got that right. It's just as well that I can out-think him a bit, or I'd never manage to keep up with him.'

'I guess that having a child puts things into perspective. You get to understand your own parents a little better.'

'Yes, it puts a lot of things into perspective. I wish that Sam could have known my dad, he would have adored him.'

'You've taught him how to fly a kite?'

Hannah laughed. 'No, actually, I haven't. That's a very good idea, though. Maybe I'll wait for a windy day and bring him up here.'

The question was on the tip of his tongue. Whether Hannah might wait for that windy day, and call him to see if he might come along. He had no idea how to fly a kite and it seemed suddenly as if it was something he'd be interested in learning about.

He didn't ask. Hannah's was one of those families that had fascinated him as a child, stable and loving, the exact opposite of his own. But they were unknown territory and he'd kept his distance. And anyway, Hannah was really just an acquaintance. One who he felt suddenly very close to, after working through the challenges they'd been set for today, but still just an acquaintance.

He jumped as someone rapped on the car window, and Hannah pressed the control to wind it down. The yellow team had been dropped off in the car park now, and were making their way to their car.

'Guys, we need you back at the hospital. We're doing a few interviews there, and when the other teams get back we'll be announcing the winners.'

'I don't suppose you know where the other teams are, do you?' Hannah's competitive spirit emerged suddenly and the young woman shook her head.

'Sorry…'

'Okay, thanks.' Hannah wound the window back up. 'Can't say or won't say, I wonder.'

Matt chuckled, reaching for the ignition. 'We'll find out soon enough.'

Hannah had stepped over the line a little. She usually gave the sanitised version of what had happened when her father had died, just that she'd been out of the country and got back as soon as she could.

She didn't tell anyone about the clawing guilt. About how she'd left, accompanying her boyfriend on travels that were his dream, not hers. John had been her dream, and she'd followed him.

Her father had asked her what she really wanted, and

she'd told him it was this. She wanted to see the world. He hadn't believed her, and he and her mother had obviously been worried for her, but they'd let her go without any more argument, waving her off at the airport with fixed smiles on their faces.

And that was the last time she'd seen him. When the telegram had got through, routed through various different post offices, she'd called her mother and found that her father was dying. John had waved her off at the airport rather more cheerfully than her parents had, and she hadn't seen him again either. By the time she'd arrived home, her father had died, and she'd never had the chance to tell him that she was sorry.

The car turned into the road that ran through to the back of the hospital and she saw her mother with Sam. He was standing right at the front of the spectator area, waving the red flag that she'd helped him make. Matt stopped the car, right in front of him.

'Mum... Mum!' Sam was hallooing at the top of his voice. Hannah shot Matt a smile and got out of the car.

'Mum... Did you win?'

'We'll have to wait for the judges to say.' Hannah stroked her son's cheek as his face fell. 'But we did the best we could, and that's what matters.'

What seemed to matter now was winning, but Sam accepted the thought without question, jumping up and down and waving his flag. Hannah gave him a hug and Sam craned around as Matt got out of the car. He gave Sam a wave and the little boy pretended not to notice, suddenly shy.

Hannah beckoned Matt over, and he walked towards them. 'Sam, this is Matt.'

'Hi, Sam.' Matt squatted down on his heels in front of the boy, giving him his space and smiling quietly as he waited for Sam to get over his attack of nerves. 'That's a great flag.'

'I made it.' Sam gave the flag another wave, and Matt nodded solemnly.

'I can see that. It's better than all the others.' He grinned when Sam waved the flag more vigorously. 'It was the first thing we saw when we got to the hospital.'

Sam liked that. He began to chatter excitedly as Matt got to his feet and introduced himself to Hannah's mum. His quiet manner, and the way he held his hand out to shake hers, elicited a glance in Hannah's direction from her mother. No doubt about the meaning—Mum liked the strong silent type, and good manners always impressed her.

The home crowd had seen them, and people were beginning to cheer, the banner with the name of the hospital lifted aloft after what must have been a long wait to greet them. Hannah lifted Sam over the barrier, feeling her fatigued muscles protest at his weight, and he waved his flag wildly.

Anxious to get as good a view as possible, Sam reached for Matt's taller frame. Hannah saw Matt hesitate, and then he smiled. As she delivered Sam into his arms, the brush of Matt's skin against hers was suddenly all she could feel. He hoisted the boy onto his shoulders, holding him carefully so that he didn't fall, and Sam howled with delight.

'He's not too heavy for you, is he?' Matt grinned a no, and Hannah tapped Sam's knee to get his attention. 'Don't wriggle so much. Matt won't be able to hold you.'

'I won't let him go.'

This. *This* was what it would be like if Sam had a father. If John had responded to the news that she was pregnant by wanting anything to do with his child. But he hadn't. He had been too busy with his own life to bother with hers or the one they'd unwittingly created together. Hannah felt a lump rise in her throat, and realised that her mother was staring at her.

'Do you mind staying here with Sam for a moment? I'll go and park the car up...' She wanted to get away from here before the picture of a complete family formed too clearly in her mind.

'Um… Yeah. Sure.' Matt clearly wasn't used to being around kids, and he was taking the responsibility seriously, but he was grinning from ear to ear. If he wanted to let Sam down, then her mum was there to take him.

'Keys…?'

'In my pocket.' Matt didn't seem at all disposed to let go of Sam, although one hand was probably quite enough to keep him from falling from his perch. Hannah saw the outline of the keys under the heavy material of his trousers, and felt her mouth go dry.

She was even thinking twice about this? She should be pleased that Matt was so careful, and that he was taking extra care that Sam didn't fall.

'Okay. Sharp…um…scratch.' The joke dried in her throat. It wasn't really necessary to warn Matt every time she went near him.

His momentary, heavy-lidded look told Hannah that he noticed her touch as much as she did his. She reached forward, fishing the keys from his pocket with two fingers, stepping back as soon as she had them, feeling the metal dig into her hand as she held them a little too tightly.

'I'm just going to park the car, Sam. You'll stay here with Matt and Grandma?' Sam gave her a cursory nod, concentrating on waving his flag.

Sophie caught up with her in the car park, flinging her arm around her shoulders as they walked back together.

'I see he's made friends with Sam. How was he?'

Beautiful. Challenging. 'Um…he's got good stamina.'

'I like a man with good stamina.' Sophie laughed and Hannah dug her elbow into her ribs.

'I meant for climbing hills. He's a good problem-solver as well.'

'Yeah? I *love* a good problem-solver…'

'Shush. If you're so keen on stamina and problem-solving, why don't you try him out for yourself?' Now she'd said it, Hannah wished she hadn't. Sophie had better *not* try Matt out for herself.

'Nah. He's all yours…' Sophie ended the conversation abruptly, jogging forward to greet Sam. 'Hey, there, Sam. You're very tall all of a sudden!'

Sam leaned over, tapping the top of Sophie's head, and she laughed.

'We'd better go and sign in. Are you going to join us, Sophie?'

Recognising that Sophie had played a part in their efforts today, and wanting her to share in the credit, was a nice gesture on Matt's part. The walk between here and the awning that covered the reception area was lined with people and they were all cheering.

'No, that's okay.' Sophie grinned conspiratorially at Hannah's mother. 'You take Sam.'

As they started to walk, she heard Sophie's voice behind her. Then the people lining their way started a Mexican wave, cheering and shouting. She heard Matt chuckle as Sam screamed with glee.

'Oh! She didn't…'

'I think she did.' Matt's voice seemed very close all of a sudden. 'One last push and we're home…'

The embarrassment, and the thought that there were so many expectations on her shoulders, made this walk seem harder, and longer than all the rest put together. Sam waved his flag, as people ducked and straightened in a new ripple that followed them all the way to the reception area. Matt lifted Sam down, and Hannah hugged him.

'Run straight back to Sophie and Grandma now, sweetie. Matt and I have to do some things, but I'll see you later.' Hannah gestured to her mother, making sure that she saw that Sam was on his way back.

'I can take him. Sign me in…' A worried look crossed Matt's face, and Hannah shook her head.

'It's okay. He can do that by himself.' Hannah watched as Sam scampered back, making sure that he didn't get distracted. Sophie took his hand, bending down to say something to him, and Sam turned, giving her a wave.

'He's great.' Matt was watching too. 'I'll bet he's a bit of a handful…'

'He's more than just a bit of a handful. But all the best kids are.'

Matt nodded thoughtfully. Then he turned suddenly, as if tearing himself away from the boy, and walked towards the signing-in table.

They'd responded to the interview questions, giving all the expected answers. They'd enjoyed the challenge, and were feeling good, and hoping they'd done well. Now that they were alone, Hannah's optimism seemed to have subsided into a worried determination. They'd reached their pretend patient first, but there was still the matter of how they'd answered the judges' questions. Matt was confident that they'd outlined the right course of action clinically speaking, but maybe they'd missed something that the other teams had seen.

Hannah was getting more and more nervous, and he tried to think of something he might say to her. There was nothing. He was nervous, too.

Taking Sam onto his shoulders had been the most challenging part of the day. Being responsible for a child, even if it was only for a few minutes and his grandmother was close by. Sam hadn't been taught to be afraid, and the way he'd clung to Matt, confident that he'd keep him safe, had been a new experience.

He shouldn't read too much into it. Hannah's mother and Sophie both looked after Sam as naturally as Hannah did. The boy was a happy, normal kid. The thought that he could be a part of what Hannah had was entirely inappropriate. And the more urgent desire to touch her was equally inappropriate.

Finally, the four teams were gathered, cameras pointing at them to record their reactions. One of the judging panel stood up and started to talk into the microphone, giving an overview of each team's performance. Hannah was standing next to Matt, looking very nervous.

'I'm taking bets on how long he's going to drag this out…' He bent, whispering into her ear behind his hand, so that the camera couldn't record his words. Even now there was a freshness about her scent that worked its way into his consciousness.

She looked up at him, smiling suddenly. 'Two minutes.'

'Okay. I'll say thirty seconds. Loser buys coffee next time round.' Matt reckoned it would be closer to three minutes. But at the moment, buying coffee for Hannah was his idea of being a winner.

She threw him a sceptical look. Matt fixed his eyes on the clock and Hannah followed suit. The second hand ticked around, and he felt her nudge him when it had signalled that two minutes had passed. He looked down at her and found that her smile was worth the price of a thousand cups of coffee.

'You win.' He murmured the words to her just as the judge's voice crashed into his consciousness.

'And the winners are… Matt and Hannah, for Hamblewell Hospital.'

Cheers erupted from the crowd, and Matt could see Sam jumping up and down, doing the victory dance he'd done with Hannah last week. Hannah seemed paralysed by the news, and he took the lead, shaking the hands of the other competitors. Matt waited until she'd followed suit, and then propelled her towards the judge.

She shook his hand, smiling and holding aloft the medal that he'd draped around her neck. Matt received his, standing next to Hannah, as everyone cheered. It was a dizzying, almost surreal experience. Winning this with Hannah was a more potent achievement than he'd thought.

An endless round of handshakes and congratulations. And then suddenly they were alone.

'Well done, Flash.'

'You too, Robin…' She frowned suddenly. 'Don't you want to be Flash? Robin sounds as if you're my sidekick…'

'Hey. You stick with your own middle name, and I'll stick with mine. I've become attached to it over the years.' He wasn't particularly attached to either of his first names, because he guessed they'd been his father's choices. But on Hannah's lips the name had acquired new and better associations.

He pulled the medal ribbon over his head. 'Would Sam like this?'

'You earned it. He can have mine.'

Matt put the medal into her hand. 'Give him this one. Then you can both wear one.' He reckoned that Sam might like that.

'Are you sure…?' Hannah looked up at him and he nodded. 'Why don't you come and give it to him yourself, so he can say thank you? We'll probably have to go for a drink somewhere before I get to go home and lie on the sofa— you're welcome to join us.'

There was nothing that Matt would like more. Being with Hannah for just a while longer. Seeing that softer side of her, which seemed to retreat behind a determined shell when she was competing. But it wasn't a good idea. He was already becoming too aware of her, and it was an uneasy path to take.

'Thanks, but I'd like to get home. I've got a few things to do.' The lie sounded hollow on his lips. 'Actually, lying on the sofa sounds like a good idea.'

Her gaze searched his face for a moment. Then she nodded. 'I'll let you go, then. Thanks for today. And the medal, Sam will love it.'

Matt watched her walk away. She knelt down in front of Sam, putting the medal around his neck, and Matt's heart began to swell as the little boy picked it up gravely, examining it. Then Hannah pointed behind her in his direction and started to turn...

He turned away quickly. It wouldn't do for her to know that he was watching, greedy for every detail of the scene. Matt walked away, starting to feel the heaviness of his limbs and the sting of the wound on his shoulder. He should go home, take a long shower, and forget all about Hannah until next week.

CHAPTER FIVE

HANNAH WAS TRYING not to think about Matt. That wasn't easy, because Sam hadn't stopped talking about him, and her mother had mentioned that he seemed nice and wondered innocently whether he had a family. Sophie didn't have such reservations.

'I asked. He's definitely single.'

Hannah leaned back in the front seat of the ambulance, closing her eyes. 'And they know this how?'

'I spoke to one of the nurses in Orthopaedics. He comes into the ward quite a lot on account of operating on quite a few of their patients.'

'Oh, and they've compiled a dossier?'

'Yeah, pretty much. He lives just around the corner from the hospital. Been here a year, isn't married and doesn't have a girlfriend, despite being a complete and utter god in the looks department.' Sophie frowned. 'That sounds a bit too good to be true actually. I wonder if he's got a dark secret.'

Hannah had wondered that too.

'Maybe he just likes to keep his personal life to himself.'

'So you know something? That you're not telling me?'

'No. We don't all have your dating stamina, I haven't had a partner in years either. I suppose that doesn't count, though, I'm not a complete and utter goddess...'

'Don't be ridiculous. You're a super-goddess.' Sophie

pulled a face. 'You just can't believe that there's someone out there who won't let you down, the way John did.'

'And I've got a six-year-old, and a job. It doesn't give me a lot of time for dating.' Hannah was sure that she could have made time if she'd really wanted to, her Mum was always telling her she should go out more. But guilt stopped her. She'd let her father down, and she wouldn't break the promise she'd never had the chance to make to him. She'd never get carried away, thinking that she was in love, and let down the people she really cared about. Her place was with Sam and her mother.

'Sure you couldn't squeeze him in?' Sophie grinned, and then puffed out a breath as the radio hissed into life.

Good. Something else to think about for a while. Something that didn't involve Matt's broad shoulders, or what might happen if a girl should accidentally-on-purpose cut through that gentle veneer of his. She'd seen the fire and the determination beneath it, and it had made her shiver.

'Here we go…' Sophie glanced at Hannah, starting the engine of the ambulance.

The second part of the competition was being held at the blue team's hospital. Matt had texted Hannah, saying that he'd be there at seven thirty, and since she'd won the bet, he would be bringing coffee. Hannah had texted him back, saying she looked forward to a latte with no sugar and her phone had pinged almost immediately with a smiley face.

Matt stood out in the crowd, and she didn't have to look for his blond hair and red T-shirt. He was next to the blue team's contingent of supporters, chatting to a girl of around thirteen in a wheelchair, who'd obviously been brought down from one of the wards to watch. Hannah walked over to him, reaching out to tap him on the shoulder, but he seemed to sense she was there before she even touched him.

'Ah, there you are.' He was holding two large cardboard

beakers and he handed one to Hannah. 'Latte, no sugar. Mia, this is Hannah.'

'Hi, Mia.' Hannah grinned down at the girl. 'You're here to cheer for the blues, are you?'

'I'm cheering for Dr Matt as well. He's my doctor.'

Matt grinned. 'Well, that's very kind of you. I'll run even faster knowing that you're watching me.' He gestured to a large screen that had been set up to one side of them. Clearly whatever they were going to be doing today would involve another location, and the cameras would be relaying what was happening.

'He'd better run if he's going to keep up with me.' Hannah shared the information with Mia and she grinned.

'That sounds a lot like a challenge.' Matt was smiling too. 'Hannah's an ambulance paramedic, Mia.'

Mia's face lit up. 'That's what I want to be…'

'It's a hard job, but I love it. I wouldn't do anything else.' Hannah wondered what was wrong with Mia and whether it would prevent her from dealing with the physical demands of the job.

'When you're better, you'll be able to do anything you want.' Matt came to her rescue. 'The ambulance service will be lucky to have you.'

'You've played a big part in making that possible.' The woman standing next to Mia was obviously her mother.

'It's been my pleasure. I'm glad to see Mia doing so well.' Matt bent down again. 'Will you come back later today?'

'You bet. I'll be cheering you and Hannah.'

Hannah grinned at her. 'Thanks. Ambulance crews have to stick together.'

They took their leave of Mia and her mother, strolling across the grass towards the reception tent. 'I didn't realise you worked here as well.'

'I operate here from time to time. Mia had severe scoliosis, which is my specialty.'

'She obviously thinks a lot of you.' In Hannah's experience you could generally judge a doctor by what their patients thought of them.

'She's a brave girl, and very determined. The first time I met her, she gave me a list—she'd written down all of the things she wanted to be able to do after her surgery.'

Hannah laughed. 'And how are you doing with that?'

'It's looking good. Mia's already working with the physiotherapists, and she's doing well. She'll tick everything off her list, given a little time.'

'It must be nice, being able to follow through with your patients. I don't always get that opportunity.'

'Some of them I don't get to know too well, on account of their being under anaesthetic. But I try to make time to see how they're doing, especially the kids. Giving them a decent start in life is…' Matt shrugged. 'It's what it's all about, really.'

Hannah nodded. She'd been lucky and had had the best start in life; whatever mistakes she'd made had been hers alone. Something about Matt told her that maybe his life had been shaped by other people's mistakes.

This time the teams were called one by one. They waited for what seemed like an age after the red team had been summoned, and finally they were kitted out with heavy boots, along with work gloves, jackets and hard hats. Then one of the production assistants ferried them by car to a row of old warehouses, empty and due for demolition. She drove away without another word, leaving them alone.

'What do we do now?' Hannah looked around. The site seemed deserted, although it was fair to assume that there must be cameras somewhere, trained on them.

'I'll walk that way a bit.' Matt gestured to his left. 'Maybe you go the other way, and see if you can see anything.'

'Okay. Stay within hollering distance.'

He nodded, walking away from her. Hannah started to walk, scanning the crumbling brick fascia of the warehouses. If the hard hat was anything to go by, they were expected to go inside one of them, but which one…?

'Hannah… This way…' She heard Matt's call, and turned, running towards him. His trajectory was more determined now, and she guessed he must have heard or seen something.

'I thought I heard someone calling out…' He was suddenly silent and Hannah heard it too. A woman's voice, shouting for help.

'I think it's coming from over there. Must be on the other side.' The voice was too faint to be coming from any of the doorways that they could see.

Matt nodded and they jogged together across the rubble-strewn ground towards the end of the row of buildings. Hannah felt her foot turn, and pain shot through her knee. Then she yelped in surprise as her downward trajectory suddenly reversed itself.

Matt had caught her, and she was pinioned against him. One arm wrapped firmly around her waist and the other hand… He moved it quickly away from the curve of her hip but it was too late. She'd already felt the pressure of his fingers.

'Um… Sorry. Are you okay?'

Maybe. Hannah wasn't quite sure. Maybe it was the sudden close-up of his blue eyes that had turned her legs to jelly, or maybe the shock of almost falling face first onto the sharp stones. Maybe that fleeting touch, but she could hardly blame him for that. Matt hadn't had the time to check exactly where he was putting his hands, and he was clearly a little embarrassed about it.

'Yes. Fine. Thanks.' He could let go of her now. Even if every fibre of her body was clamouring for his.

He nodded, hesitating for just one moment before he stepped away from her. In that moment, Hannah could have sworn that he felt it too. The heat of an attraction that stubbornly failed to respond to reason. Matt turned to retrieve her hard hat, which had spun out of her hand, landing some feet away.

Her knee hurt. But she could keep going. 'You go on ahead, I'll catch you up.'

'I'll wait.' There was no trace of impatience in his tone.

He was right, they should stay together, and Sophie would have done the exact same thing in these circumstances. But when Matt did it, all Hannah could think about was that she'd had no more than a taste of his strong arms, and she wanted more. She tried to concentrate on her knee, flexing her leg, and the pain subsided a little. When she took a couple of steps it felt better still.

'I'm good.' She started to walk again, and Matt fell into step beside her, still watching her. When they reached the other side of the warehouses, which faced the road, the voice became louder and clearer.

'Up there.' Matt was the first to see it. A flash of red at one of the upper windows. As they ran closer they could see it was a woman waving a red scarf.

'Are you okay?' Hannah shouted up to her. The woman was making a great job of appearing panicked and distressed.

'I'm all right. My boyfriend… He's hurt…' The woman seemed about to climb out of the window.

'Stay there. Don't try to climb down, we'll come to you. What's your name?' Matt was already on his way towards the door, leaving Hannah to deal with the woman.

'Isobel. You can't get up here…'

'Okay, Isobel. Leave that to us. Are you safe where you are right now?'

'Yes.'

'Can you see your boyfriend?' Hannah knew that when dealing with someone who was panicking and probably in shock, she had to give clear, step-by-step instructions.

'Yes…'

'Listen to me carefully, Isobel. Put your hand on the windowsill.' Isobel hesitated, but she did it. 'Good. Now turn and look at him. Tell me what you see.'

'He fell… There's blood and I think he's broken his leg.'

'Is he breathing?'

'Yes…'

'What does his breathing sound like, can you hear a rasping sound?'

'No, he's breathing easily.'

Hopefully so. 'That's good, Isobel. Have you got a phone on you?'

Hannah waited while Isobel did as she was bidden. Where was Matt? He should be up there by now, but she suspected that was going to be far too easy a solution. He appeared again at the door, running towards her.

'The way up there is blocked with rubble. We're going to have to dig our way through.' He glanced up at the window, where Isobel was watching them. 'Do you have an idea of the situation?'

'I've got pictures. Or I will have…' Hannah's phone beeped, and she opened the texts that Isobel had sent. The pictures showed a large open space, and a lifelike dummy with a good representation of a broken leg. There must be a wound as well, because blood was pooling on the floor. Isobel had obviously been well drilled in giving answers that matched the scenario, and this felt chillingly real.

Matt scrolled through the pictures. 'We need to get up there as fast as we can. We're going to have to hope that Isobel doesn't decide to start panicking again. I'll need your help to clear the debris.' The scenario obviously felt real to him as well.

'Maybe we can improvise. Perhaps there's something we can use as a tool, rather than digging with our hands.' Hannah looked around.

They were near the perimeter of the site, where the warehouses were separated from the pavement by a chain-link fence. On the other side of the road was a row of shops, and a group of men was fixing a new fascia sign to one of them. Their aerial work platform, mounted on the back of a truck, caught Hannah's attention.

'Do you think we could reach the window with that?'

Matt studied the vehicle for a moment and then, before Hannah could stop him, he made for the fence and began to scale it. It bent a little under his weight as he hauled himself over the top, twanging back into shape when he jumped down on the other side.

'Hey…!' A little discussion might have been nice.

'What?' Matt spread his hands in a querying gesture. 'It's a great idea.'

'What if they're nothing to do with the challenge? Are we allowed to ask for their help?'

'Wouldn't you and Sophie, if this were real?'

He had a point. Hannah sighed, turning back to Isobel and calling up to her to stay where she was until they could reach her. When she glanced behind her she saw that Matt was talking to the men, and they were retracting the aerial lift work platform. Matt got into the passenger seat of the truck and it drove away.

Five minutes later, the truck bumped across the service road at the back of the warehouses. The driver parked under the window, and Matt and Hannah climbed onto the aerial platform, donning their helmets.

'What did you tell them?' Hannah whispered the words as the platform began to rise towards the window.

'I said this was a challenge, which was being filmed for TV, and that we were competing for Hamblewell Hospital. They were more than happy to give it a go.'

Fair enough. Matt had turned his attention to directing the driver exactly where to place the platform. As soon as it was level with the window, he helped Hannah inside the building, making straight for the figure lying on the floor, while Hannah took a moment to calm Isobel.

The exercise hadn't been just an exercise. It had made Matt think. Would he be a better surgeon now, having faced the kind of situations that ambulance crews had to contend with?

They'd rigged up a makeshift splint and bandages, and ferried Isobel and their patient back down to the ground. As soon as she stepped off the platform, Isobel broke character, smilingly telling them that the challenge was now finished, and a couple of cars appeared to ferry them back to the hospital.

It would be at least two hours before they were needed again. That was good, because Matt had something urgent on his mind.

'What's the matter with your leg? You're limping…'

'Am I?' Hannah turned her mouth down, as if he hadn't been meant to notice.

'Yeah. I'll take a look…' There was no point in going through the toing and froing of Hannah denying there was anything wrong, and him telling her that he knew there was. It was only the long route to an outcome that he'd already decided on.

'It's nothing. I just twisted it a bit when I fell. Don't make a fuss, Matt.'

Making a fuss was a tempting prospect at the moment. But his childhood had taught him that conflict was no way to reconcile a disagreement. Matt swallowed his annoyance and tried logic instead.

'You're my teammate. I need you in full working order for next week.'

That silenced her. She followed him into the hospital building, and Matt ignored her frown as he took the lift up to the orthopaedic department. A quick enquiry of one of the doctors that he knew elicited access to one of the treatment rooms, and he ushered Hannah inside.

'This is entirely unnecessary. Do you think I can't do this for myself?'

'I'm sure you can. Since you haven't yet, I'll do it for you. Like I said, I need you to keep up with me...'

That did it. She sat down on the couch, unlacing her boots and letting them fall to the floor with a clunk. Red socks. Matt studiously ignored the fact that they seemed somehow special and delightful when worn by Hannah. When she swung her legs up onto the couch, he quickly snatched up a pillow and placed it at the other end for her head.

'Comfortable?'

'No.' She glowered at him. Clearly she'd prefer to be somewhere else right now. 'I'm not your patient, Matt.'

So that was what was bothering her. Hannah was far more comfortable with being invincible, and just taking him along with her for the ride. Irritation started to prickle his skin, and he took a step back, putting his hands into his pockets. The one thing that he could never be, with Hannah, was indifferent. He had to own that, and ignore the impulse to provoke an equal reaction from her. He was a doctor, and acting that way would be good right now.

'All right.' He gave her his best doctor-patient smile. 'Point one. You *have* hurt yourself and someone needs to take a look at it. Getting yourself in the right position to examine your own knee properly isn't easy, I've tried it.'

She stared at him. Clearly Hannah took the point, and Matt decided to move on.

'Point two, I'm an orthopaedic surgeon. Which means I'm qualified.'

'Over-qualified, I'd say.' Hannah still wasn't going to give up. Neither was Matt.

'Point three. I'm your teammate. When are you going to start trusting me?'

He'd hit a nerve. Hannah sat up on the couch, grimacing at him.

'Are you telling me that our partnership isn't working for you?'

It worked just fine. He was aware of Hannah watching him carefully from time to time—most of the time actually—but it still worked. 'It *could* work a little better.'

He knew that look. It was the wary, thoughtful look of someone who had been hurt.

'And you think that's *my* fault?'

He shook his head. His father had blamed everyone else for his own shortcomings and that was something that Matt didn't want to emulate.

'No, it's *our* fault. Mine as well. I think that we're both people who like to manage things on our own, and that we both have difficulty in trusting others. That usually works pretty well for both of us, but the whole point of this competition is to take us out of our comfort zones.'

She was thinking about it. Hannah was either going to roll her trouser leg up and let him take a look at her knee, or she was going to get off the couch, grab her boots and limp off down the corridor.

Her lip curled, and she reached for the leg of her trousers, folding the material carefully as she pulled it up.

'You'll be wanting to see the other knee. To compare.' She reached for the other trouser leg, rolling that up too. Matt wondered if he should congratulate her on anticipating his next move, and decided that she might not take that too well.

'Thank you.' He stepped forward, looking at both knees carefully.

'I don't see any swelling, I'm going to check the movement... Tell me when it hurts.'

She nodded, and Matt carefully bent her leg, watching her face intently. Maybe he should trust Hannah enough to just tell him when there was any pain...

Or not. He saw it in her face but she said nothing.

'That hurts?'

'A little.'

'Okay, how about that?' He moved the leg again, checking the ligaments on the other side of her knee.

'No, that's fine.'

'And this…?' He dug his thumb into the side of her knee, and she shook her head. That was good. Matt moved on to the spot that ought to hurt, and she winced.

'Yeah. That's a little tender.'

He nodded. 'And what's your diagnosis?'

Hannah smirked. 'You're the expert. You tell me.'

Matt gave her a small smile. 'I'd say it's an injury to the medial collateral ligament. Grade One so it shouldn't give you too much trouble. Treatment?'

She gave him an argumentative look. 'Don't patronise me. I may not be a doctor, but I'm fully aware that rest, ice, compression and support should sort it. I'll be okay by next week.'

He rose to the challenge. 'It should be improved. It'll be a few weeks before the knee is back up to full strength.'

'Right. I stand corrected, Mr Lawson.'

'And I'll know that I need to compensate for you a bit.'

She didn't like that one bit. Hannah flashed him a look that left him in no doubt that she was contemplating jumping off the couch and strangling him.

'Just as you might like to compensate for me,' Matt added, quickly.

'Compensate how?' Hannah had obviously decided to put the strangling on hold for a moment.

'Getting help from those men with the aerial lift truck was a great idea. But I got the distinct impression that you thought I was jumping the gun…'

She looked at him steadily. 'And were you?'

He may as well admit it. 'Yes, I was. I reckoned I'd climb the fence before you had a chance to try it. You were already limping and I'm not sure you would have made it with that knee.'

Hannah grinned suddenly. 'You're probably right. But a bit more communication would have been nice.'

'Point taken. Can I trust you to remind me if I forget that?'

'Oh, yes, I'll remind you.' Hannah thought for a moment. 'Can I trust you to pick me up if I fall over again?'

Matt chuckled. 'Yeah. Any time.'

Trust wasn't something he usually shared with people he didn't know well. But he and Hannah had to become a team if they were going to win the prize for their hospital. *Hannah's* hospital. He might be moving on soon.

Matt dismissed the thought of the job application forms, lying on his desk at home. That was the future, and as ever he was uncertain about where he'd be a few months from now. This was now.

'Would you like to come back and have dinner with us afterwards?' Hannah's question broke his reverie. 'Sophie's bringing Sam along to see the results announced, and Mum's making burgers, she always makes a few extra and puts them in the freezer so there's plenty to go round. We could talk tactics for next week.'

It wasn't the kind of invitation he usually accepted. But getting to know Hannah better was the obvious precursor to building trust and teamwork.

'Thanks. That would be great. I'll go and see if I can rustle up some ice and a light knee support. Why don't you stay here?'

She nodded. Then she smiled suddenly. 'Did you miss something?'

Matt chuckled. 'You mean did I miss telling you that your knee is just fine, and apart from a slight injury you have good movement and excellent muscle tone? Or the part about the small ganglion cyst on the side of your knee?'

'So you *did* find it? What were you thinking, that you wouldn't mention it?'

'I didn't want to sound like a know-all. I reckoned you must be aware of it, and I'm sure you also know that it might well disappear on its own, without any treatment. I don't imagine it hurts.'

'No, it doesn't. It's nice to know that you caught it, though.' Hannah gave him a brilliant smile, and Matt smirked back.

'Now that we have that cleared up, I'll go and get the ice. Stay put.'

He'd wanted to protect her. Matt had wanted to be nice to Hannah, and not make her feel that he was criticising or second-guessing her, the way his father had with his mother. But he'd been doing it all wrong. A woman like Hannah, and maybe a man like him, thrived on straight-forwardness and honesty.

'All right. Hurry up, we don't have all day.'

CHAPTER SIX

THE CHEMISTRY BETWEEN Hannah and her new teammate had undeniably been growing, and even though she'd tried to ignore it, Hannah had to admit to herself that she enjoyed it. Maybe that, along with a fierce desire to keep up with whatever pace Matt set, was why she'd fought so hard when he'd suggested he examine her knee.

But as soon as he'd walked into the consulting room, he'd changed. No less confronting, but he was cool and professional. Hannah let Matt place the ice on her knee, and sat patiently until he told her that would do for the time being. Then he wrapped a soft support around her leg, checking that it didn't hamper her movement but that it was tight enough to aid the healing process.

'I thought I'd go along to the orthopaedic ward and see Mia. You want to come?'

'Yes. They won't mind that we're not their team?'

'We're on their team, in every way that counts. There are a lot of ambitions in that ward, and we're the ones who are working to help them achieve those ambitions.'

It was a nice way of putting it. 'That's what makes you want to win?'

'One of the things.'

He led the way to the ward, and when he and Hannah entered there was a small murmur of excitement. She saw Mia waving from the far end, and when the ward sister nodded in response to Matt's request that they might spend some time here, she walked over to her.

'How did you do?'

'Hmm. Not sure. We did our best.'

'That's all you can do.' Mia spoke with a wisdom beyond her years and Hannah suspected that it was what Matt and the rehab specialists had told her.

'Would you like to hear about it? We had a rescue situation, a bit like the ones that you can come across, working as ambulance crew. We had to deal with it on our own, though usually an ambulance crew has back-up from the other rescue services.'

'You bet I want to hear about it.' Mia's eyes were shining.

Hannah heard Matt's quiet chuckle behind her. 'I'll leave you to it. Would you ladies like some juice?'

Mia nodded, and Hannah grinned at him. 'Hey, we're not ladies. What are we, Mia?' She turned to Mia, mouthing the answer.

'We're ambos!'

'My mistake. I'll get you two ambos some juice.'

Matt had left her with Mia while he worked his way around the ward, talking to the other kids. He had a nice way with them, and they were obviously relaxed and confident in his company. Hannah reckoned he must spend a lot more time here on the ward than his job required.

She ended up talking to Mia for over an hour, answering her questions, without being too blunt about the distressing parts of her job. It was clear that this was part of the dream that kept Mia going through all of the pain and the distress of her condition.

'We have to get going now. Sorry, Mia.' Matt returned, shooting Mia an apologetic look.

'That's okay. Thanks, Hannah.'

'My pleasure. I'll pop in again, and let you know what other scrapes Dr Matt has got himself into.'

'Oh, really?' Matt feigned outrage and Mia giggled. 'Next time Hannah gets herself into a scrape, I'll make sure to take a picture and send it to you…'

They walked out of the ward together, and back down to the area where the outside broadcast trucks were parked. It felt as if it would have been almost natural to take Matt's hand. As if they were close, in a way they hadn't been when they'd arrived back here. That wasn't appropriate, though, or wise. The alternate reality, where she and Matt could be *that* close, didn't exist. There was only this world, and in this world Hannah didn't take chances.

They waited, and Hannah went across to greet Sam when he arrived with Sophie. The crowd grew, along with the obvious tension amongst the contestants, all waiting to see who was going to be the winner.

'I reckon they dug their way through…' Matt nudged her, nodding towards the green team, whose T-shirts were covered in grime.

'Maybe that's what we were all supposed to do.' Hannah turned the corners of her mouth down. They'd solved the problem, making use of the resources at their disposal. In the real world you didn't question your luck, or the presence of the right person at the right time.

'We'll see.' Matt took a deep breath as they were all gestured up onto the podium.

There was the inevitable wait as microphones were tested and the judges got ready to announce their decision. Hannah saw Sam in the crowd and waved to him. Mia was amongst the home supporters, with her mother, talking excitedly.

Then a judge stepped forward. She congratulated all of the teams, going through what had caught the judges' eyes about each of them. The truck *had* been put there by the TV company to see if any of the contestants would spot it and ask for help. Hannah waited, trying to keep her face from betraying her thoughts.

'And now for the winners. For the second time—it's Matt and Hannah…'

A roar went up from the crowd, drowning out the rest of what she was saying. And suddenly, without thinking, all the pent-up emotion burst through and she was in Matt's arms.

There was nothing else. Just his arms around her, and the feeling that she wanted to get closer, to touch his skin. Hannah couldn't help letting out a sigh, as she felt herself melt against him.

'Way to go, Robin.' She felt his lips brush her cheek, a thrilling second that should have lasted longer.

'You too, Flash.'

Then he let her go. They shook hands with the other contestants, and Matt took her hand, leading her up to the judge to receive her medal. Hannah waved to the cheering crowd, unable to look at him but powerless to stop thinking about the feel of his strong body.

Hannah was still limping slightly as she hurried across the grass towards Sophie and Sam, but her knee was clearly less painful than it had been. Matt watched as she hugged Sam, and they did their victory dance. He wanted her so much he could hardly breathe.

Hannah was in conversation with Sam, and it seemed to be about something important. Sam was nodding, and Hannah hugged him, and then stood up as Sophie took his hand to walk towards the ice-cream van that was parked in the car park behind them. Then Hannah began to walk along the line of spectators, looking for someone.

He knew what she was about to do, just as surely as if she'd shouted her intentions over her shoulder at him. Hannah walked along the line of kids who had been brought down from the wards to watch, and Matt jogged across the grass towards her. He wanted to see this.

She knelt down opposite Mia, who was talking excitedly. Then Hannah took off her medal, hanging it carefully around Mia's neck.

'Hannah, are you sure…?' Mia's mother spoke up.

'Of course. Mia deserves this.' She grinned down at Mia, who was clutching the medal to her chest, just in case her mother decided to try and take it away from her. 'What you're doing now is hard, Mia. But if you can do all that Dr Matt and the physiotherapist tell you, then you can do anything.'

Matt wanted to hug her again. He wanted to feel her body against his, and this time it wasn't just a heat of the moment thing. He'd thought about it and he *needed* to hug her. Instead he smiled at Mia's mother.

'What about a photograph?'

'Oh, yes, of course.' Mia's mother began to rummage in her handbag, and Mia produced her own phone from her pocket. 'Give it to me, darling, and we can take one with Hannah and Dr Matt.'

The photos were taken, and then Matt saw one of the nurses beckoning him over. 'Will Sam mind if we stay a minute for some more photos?'

'No, Sophie's promised him an ice cream and from the looks of the queue they'll be a little while.' She smiled. 'I asked him if he'd mind me giving my medal to a girl who was sick and had been very brave, and he told me that was the right thing to do.'

Matt chuckled. 'That was kind of him.'

'He has his moments. He surprises me all the time, though, he's starting to think about things. I found him tipping the contents of the bin out on the kitchen floor the other day. They'd given them all a talk about recycling at school, and he told me that Grandma wasn't doing it properly.'

'Good for him. It's his future.' Matt felt a lump form in his throat. Sam didn't just know what was right, Hannah had taught him. He knew only love, and he understood that other kids weren't as lucky as he was.

'Let's take some photos, then…' She smiled up at him, striding across to a little boy who was waving to them, telling the child next to him to be patient and he'd get a photo too. Matt joined her, kneeling down next to the boy's wheelchair and smiling for the camera.

The other teams had seen what they were doing and had joined in, posing for photographs with the children. Hannah was chatting to the last little girl when Matt saw Sophie walking towards them, balancing two ice-cream cones in one hand. Sam was dawdling along next to her, intent on demolishing his own ice cream as quickly as possible before it melted.

'Hi, Matt. You and Hannah did a great job today. Four points ahead on the leader board.'

'Thanks. It was mainly Hannah…' He might have helped things along, but it was Hannah who had inspired him. Who'd made him want to win more than anything.

'Well, you deserve an ice cream at least.' Sophie proffered one of the cones she was carrying and when he hesitated she gave an impatient nod. 'Take it. I'll share with Hannah.'

The ice cream was cool in his mouth and welcome on a hot summer's day like today. Matt bent down, squatting on his heels in front of Sam.

'Hey, little man. I have something for you.' He took the medal from around his neck, and put it around Sam's. The little boy regarded it steadily.

'Look at that! I think Matt deserves a thank-you, don't you, Sam?' Sophie nudged Sam's shoulder.

'Thank you.' Sam took Matt by surprise, suddenly flinging his arms around his neck, depositing the last of the ice cream from his cone on the back of Matt's T-shirt. Then he ran over to Hannah, showing her the medal, and she turned, her eyes bright. Matt would have given anything to receive that one look.

She mouthed a thank-you, and Matt nodded.

'I think that warrants a photograph.' Sophie gave the last ice-cream cone to Hannah and took her phone from her pocket. Hannah came to stand next to him, her shoulder touching his, and Sam stood in front, leaning against Matt's legs. They could almost have been a happy family. Matt longed to put his arm around Hannah.

The moment was captured, but didn't last long enough. He'd watched Hannah and Sam together, and seen her ice-queen mask slip when she was with her son. And now, for just a little while, he was a part of it all. Matt had told himself that it was impossible to miss what you'd never had, and for the most part he believed it. Right now, the ache of knowing that they were just posing for the camera was almost unbearable.

'Are we ready to go?' Hannah bent down towards Sam. 'It's burgers tonight, your favourite. Aunt Sophie and Matt are coming with us as well.'

'Hooray!' Sam careened around in a circle, and Hannah smiled.

'Right, then. Hungry mouths to feed…'

Matt followed Sophie's car to one of the small villages that bordered Hamblewell. The house was set a little way back from the road and surrounded by a neat garden, the russet-coloured bricks blending in with the flowers and climbing plants around the doorway.

There were already two cars parked in the driveway, but Sophie manoeuvred in beside them with only inches to spare, leaving the space outside in the road clear for Matt to park. He saw Hannah lean back, undoing Sam's seat belt, and he tumbled out of the car, running towards the front door.

'Grandma… Grandma!' He shouted through the letter box. 'Mum and Matt won! They're ahead of everyone else!'

Hannah's mother opened the door, and Sam tumbled inside. She greeted Matt, and hugged Hannah, obviously enjoying the sudden influx of noise and laughter. Hannah showed Matt through a large, comfortable sitting room to a shaded patio at the back of the house.

'Sit down. I'll go and get some drinks.' Hannah disappeared through the open door of the kitchen, and the sound of voices erupted. She backed out of the kitchen, holding her hands up in a gesture of surrender, and Matt heard Sam's voice.

'Go away, Mum. We're cooking!'

'Okay, sweetheart. I'll leave you to it. I love you,' Hannah called in through the open door, and turned back towards Matt. 'Apparently drinks will be brought out to us. The kitchen's out of bounds.'

Matt sank into the cushions of the wooden patio chairs. 'That's nice. I could do with a rest.'

'Me too.' Hannah grinned, sitting down and unlacing her boots. She stripped off her socks, wiggling her toes as she stretched her legs out in front of her.

Sophie appeared with two glasses and a jug of iced lemonade, setting them down beside Hannah on the table and producing an ice pack from under her arm. 'Which one of you needs this?'

'Me. Thanks.' Hannah reached up, taking the ice pack and applying it to her knee. 'It's okay.'

'You're sure? I've heard your version of *okay* before.'

'Matt took a look at it. Grade One MCL injury.' Hannah pulled her trouser leg up, unwrapping the knee support. 'See I've even got this…'

Sophie nodded her approval, pulling one of the other chairs around so that Hannah could prop her leg up on it. 'Don't let her move, Matt.'

'Right you are.' Matt grinned as Sophie disappeared

back into the kitchen. This was nice. The rough and tumble of a loving family home.

Hannah leaned forward, pouring the lemonade and handing Matt a glass. She took a couple of mouthfuls of her own drink and then settled back into her seat, obviously tired out.

'Have you always lived here?' The sitting room had the quiet air of an established home.

Hannah shook her head. 'No, my parents lived right out in the sticks. I'd moved into a flat in town to be closer to the hospital while I was training, and then I took a year out to travel. When my dad died, my mum decided that she wanted to move into town so that she was less isolated. I was pregnant, and we decided to get this place together. It suited us both.'

'It must be great for Sam. To have his grandmother so close.'

'It's great for me, too. Sophie and I work the early shift, so Mum gets Sam up and takes him to school and then I'm there to pick him up.' She smiled lazily. 'Mum's joined a book club *and* the local women's guild. She's a busy women these days.'

'Not so much at first, then? After your father died?'

'No. My dad was her whole world. It took a while before she was able to pick herself up again when he died.'

Supporting her mother through her grief, *and* looking after a child on her own. It can't have been easy for Hannah. Maybe her fierce determination had been forged in that fire. 'It must have been difficult for you, too.'

Her finger started to tap on the side of her glass, the rhythm suggesting stress. 'I made my mistakes. Not being there when my dad died. Getting pregnant with someone who didn't want to know.'

'You were just…living your life, weren't you?'

Hannah gave a dry laugh. 'I'd feel better about it if I had been. I'm not sure that I actually *was* living my life, my ambitions were always to go into medicine. I was just blindly following someone who turned out to be the wrong guy.'

Matt knew he was the wrong guy, too. He had a lot in common with Sam's father, he couldn't stay in one place for too long, and he didn't know how to take on the responsibility of being a father. A concerned and dedicated doctor was about as much commitment as he could manage.

He had no answer for Hannah. But she smiled suddenly, providing her own.

'We live and learn, though. I know that I belong here.'

'It's a good place to belong.' A great place. Hannah had attained her ambitions work-wise and she was raising a happy little boy who wasn't afraid of the world.

Sam ran out of the kitchen, wearing a super-hero apron. He flung himself across Hannah's legs, dislodging the ice-pack which slithered onto the decking.

'Aunt Sophie says I've got to come and see if you're moving.'

'Well, you can tell her I'm staying absolutely still.' Hannah smiled, stroking her son's hair.

'I mixed the burgers.' Sam decided that he should report on his own progress.

'Did you? I can't wait to taste them.'

Sam nodded sagely. 'Aunt Sophie's got to cook them first or they'll make you ill. You'll have to wait.'

'Yes, I dare say I will. Did you wash your hands?'

'Yes.' Sam held out his hands, and Hannah went through the motions of inspecting them. Then he scooted back into the kitchen, clearly not wanting to miss anything that was going on in there.

'So… Are we good for next week?' Sam had broken the train of thought that had been carrying Matt to the inevitable conclusion that he would never be able to touch Hannah in the way he wanted to. That was just as well, it was better not to even consider the prospect.

'We're good.' She flashed him a mischievous smile.

'Since I'm not supposed to move, I can't pick that ice-pack up, can I?'

Matt went to stand, then leaned back in his seat, realising that Hannah was teasing him. 'It's a therapeutic measure. I'll give you a special dispensation.'

She snorted with laughter, leaning forward and grabbing the ice-pack from the ground, gesturing towards him with it as if she were about to lay it on his skin, and Matt chuckled. Hannah was enchanting, and he couldn't help wanting to know her better. Wanting to feel her again, hugging him as they won another victory together. If he had to wait another week for that, then patience was his new best friend.

CHAPTER SEVEN

THERE WAS A subtle difference in the way that Hannah greeted him the following Saturday. Something had changed.

They were both still nervously anticipating what the day might hold. But they were a team now. Ready to push each other to the limit, instead of just pushing themselves. The competitors were sent to separate rooms on the ground floor of the yellow team's hospital, and after a few minutes a production assistant entered.

'One of you is to come with me.'

Which one? Before Matt could volunteer to go, Hannah spoke.

'I'll go.'

He swallowed down the questions about whether her knee was all right now, and if he shouldn't be the one to pave the way. Hannah was fearless, and she wanted to be first.

'Okay.' He smiled at her. 'Good luck with it. Whatever it is.'

He felt a sinking feeling as he watched her walk out of the room, and the door closed behind her. Up till now, he'd wanted to face the odds and succeed. Today he wanted to face the odds with Hannah at his side. Matt sat down, leaning forward to plant his elbows on his knees and staring at the floor. Waiting, keeping his focus, was a part of his job. He knew how to do that.

Ten minutes later the door opened again, and he jumped to his feet. Hannah appeared, and he scanned her quickly for any signs of what she'd been doing. She was holding two safety helmets in her hand.

'It's an obstacle course. We have to do it together.'

'Okay.' They'd both done an obstacle course before, that shouldn't be too much of a problem.

'Only I have to guide you.' She gave him one of the helmets and Matt inspected it. There was an earpiece, which he assumed was linked to the microphone on Hannah's helmet. And his also incorporated a pair of black-out goggles, which would render him completely sightless. Matt swallowed hard.

'All right. Anything you want to say to me while I can still see you?' Perhaps they could quickly work out some kind of code—anything that might help them.

She smiled suddenly. 'Good luck, Robin. I'll be there with you every step of the way.'

Matt decided that the best thing he could take with him was Hannah's smile. He took one last, long look, and put the goggles over his eyes, rendering himself completely blind. He felt Hannah carefully checking that everything was in place, and then her fingers brushed his cheek.

'I can't touch you either. Not after we get out of this room. We both have to get across six obstacles.'

'Both of us?' That meant that Hannah was going to have to do the course, and guide him as well.

'Yes. It's going to be tricky. If I tell you to freeze, just stay where you are. I'll be working out our next move. But I'll be there, all the time.'

'I know...' He suddenly felt helpless, totally reliant on Hannah. It was both terrifying and exciting.

'Let's give it a go. Can you hear me okay through the earpiece?'

'Yep.'

'Good. Turn thirty degrees right, and then take three paces. The door will be right in front of you.'

Even that small obstacle was difficult, and he took two goes to get it right. Hannah was quiet and patient, and he began to rely on her voice. The soft scent of her body became suddenly more prominent, and he tried to resist it. But sinking into it, allowing it to reassure him, gave him confidence. As she guided him carefully around the room he began to move more steadily.

The sound of the door opening, followed by a woman's voice. 'Ready…?'

'Yes, we're ready.' He felt Hannah's fingers curling around his in one last touch that was overwhelming in its intensity. 'Stick with me, eh?'

'Like glue.' Someone checked his helmet and then took his arm and led him slowly out of the building. He felt the caress of a breeze on his cheek and grass under his feet, and heard a cheer from the red team's supporters. Then a loudspeaker called for silence, and he was turned around a couple of times, leaving him dizzy and disorientated. Then Hannah's voice. The only thing he had to cling onto.

'Ready to go?'

'Give me a minute.' Matt took a deep breath, steadying himself. He imagined Hannah's smile in front of him, and the world began to stop its frantic whirl. 'I'm ready.'

An almost eerie silence had fallen across the supporters, as four teams started to make their way towards the four identical sets of obstacles that faced them. Matt needed all of her attention and all of her concentration.

'There are six obstacles. The first is stepping stones. Six paces ahead of us…'

He followed her instructions. Hannah put her foot on the first stepping stone, feeling it spring slightly. 'There's a bit of movement in the stones. When you put your weight on it, it sinks down.'

That was bound to disorient him. But Matt was letting her guide him, and they cleared the stones without any mishaps. When she glanced across at the blue team, she saw that one of them had fallen, and they were back at the start again.

'How are the others doing?' Matt muttered quietly to her.

'Forget about them. It's just us...' Just them and a couple of hundred other people, all standing silently so that the teams could hear each other. But Matt had to concentrate, and she had to be his only reality at the moment. The thought elicited a quiver, deep in her stomach.

She saw his lips curve and he nodded. 'How many steps to the next one?'

'I'd say about ten. Keep going until I tell you to stop...'

They made their way carefully across the hanging loops, Matt's strength allowing him to go slowly and let Hannah tell him where the next hand-hold was. The water slide was easier, and Matt did it almost without any guidance, just a reassurance when they got to the top that he could allow himself to slide down the other side. A tangle of elastic ropes proved unexpectedly difficult and Matt got snagged up in them, but Hannah talked him through. They were ahead of the other teams, and she wondered whether he could hear the excitement in her voice.

Then she put a foot wrong. She was keeping her eye on Matt and landed awkwardly as she jumped down from the climbing net. Pain shot through her knee and she gasped.

'Hannah...?' He was standing quite still, his hand moving to the strap of his helmet. He knew she was in trouble, and any moment now he was going to take it off so that he could come to her aid.

'Don't... Keep the helmet on...' Hannah resisted the temptation to tell him that she was all right. She'd done that last time, and he'd known it was a lie. 'My knee hurt a bit when I jumped down. It's not too bad, I can finish. You can look at it then.'

'Tell me if it gets worse…'

'Sure…' He didn't move. 'I promise. Now get going…'

She took a couple of steps and found that the pain was subsiding, her knee strengthened by the support that she wore. The last, and most challenging, of the obstacles was still ahead of them.

The climbing wall had to be fifteen feet high, and was surrounded by air-filled cushions. It seemed almost impossible, towering above them.

'This is the last one.'

He must have heard the tremor in her voice. Matt nodded, his lips forming a thin line. 'Let's do it.'

She managed to guide him up the first ten feet, climbing by his side. Then, concentrating on where Matt should reach, she missed one of her own footholds, slithering back down before she could grab on again.

'Hannah!'

'I'm okay. Wait…'

He waited, stock still, while she climbed back up again. By the time she reached him, she felt as if she were nearing the brick wall that all athletes slammed into at one time or another.

'Stop a minute. Catch your breath.' He must have heard her ragged breaths through the earpiece, and that wasn't a request, it was a command. Hannah settled herself firmly on two good footholds, clinging to the wall and laying her head against its surface. The short climb to the top seemed suddenly impossible.

He was skimming his fingers across the wall, finding his next handhold. Slowly, he hauled himself up, his foot searching for a secure support. He was climbing blind, and Hannah could only watch, wishing that she had his strength.

'How much further?'

'Five feet.' It seemed like five miles.

'One step at a time, then.'

That sounded great. In principle. 'I don't think I can...'

'Don't think about it, just do it. Move!'

This was so different from the way he'd wordlessly picked up her bag, refusing to goad her into trying harder. But Matt was right there, with exactly what she needed right now.

Suddenly she was strong again. 'Damn you, Robin!' She reached for the next handhold and found it.

'Get a move on, Flash...'

He was grinning now, and Hannah couldn't help a grim smile. Together they climbed to the top of the wall.

'It's a shallow slide back down. Then about fifty metres to the finishing line.'

'Got it. You go first.'

Hannah struggled to pull herself over the top of the wall, sliding gratefully down the shallow incline on the other side. Matt was still at the top, automatically looking around in an instinctive attempt to orientate himself.

'Matt... Follow my voice.' She called up to him and he turned his head towards her, then pointed directly at her. 'That's right. You're facing in the right direction, just climb over the top and slide down.'

They stumbled across the finishing line together. Matt fell to his knees, and Hannah reached for him, unbuckling the chin strap of his helmet so that he could take it off. As he blinked in the sunlight, she finally allowed herself to sink down onto the grass.

'Is your knee okay?' He sat down on the grass next to her.

'It's throbbing a bit. It only hurts as much as the rest of me.'

Matt chuckled, seeming content to take her word for it. 'How did we do?'

'We were neck and neck with the blues, I wouldn't like

to make the call. We were well in the lead, but I slowed us up a bit on the last obstacle.'

'You did a great job. That wasn't as easy as it seemed.' He grinned at her.

'You too.' Hannah held out her hand to give him a high five. It wasn't the empty gesture that it might have been at the start of this competition. When their palms touched, he laced his fingers together with hers, gripping her hand in an expression of triumph. Something else as well. There was tenderness in his face, and when his gaze met hers it held her breathless in its thrall. One moment of exquisite closeness.

A cry sounded behind them, and they both looked round. Laura, the blindfolded partner for the yellow team, had fallen from the slide on the other side of the climbing wall. Her partner Jack had waved the first-aid team away, bending down beside her and talking intently. Then she got up slowly, and started to walk uncertainly towards the finish line.

The greens were trailing behind, but beginning to catch up now. A murmur ran around the crowd and the production assistants standing in front of them all motioned for quiet. Matt stood up, holding out his hand, and Hannah felt his strength boost her onto her feet.

The greens were closing, but Laura made it across the finishing line first, collapsing into Jack's arms. There was a moment of silence as he lowered her to the ground and took her helmet off, obviously concerned about her. Then he gave a thumbs-up to the crowd. Matt started to clap, and the other teams joined in. The applause caught in the breeze, spreading through the audience.

The yellows waved, and a cheer went up. The director was hurrying over to them, obviously concerned, and after a brief conversation he picked up a microphone.

'Laura's okay…' He paused as a ripple of applause ran around the crowd. 'We're going to break now until after lunch, and we'll have the second challenge ready at two o'clock.'

'There's *another* one?' Hannah grimaced up at Matt.

'So it seems. I hope it involves sitting down.' He grinned, stretching his limbs, and started to walk towards where Hannah's mum was standing with Sam.

Her mum had apparently been texting Matt, and had already elicited an agreement from him to join them for lunch. They found a shaded spot at the edge of the area that had been set aside for today's event, and her mother unpacked the sandwiches, while Matt went to his car to fetch the drinks. There was a chilled bottle of sparkling, non-alcoholic cordial, so that Sam could share their toast to a continued run of success.

'Where on earth does he get the energy?' Matt had talked with her mother about the book that she was currently reading with her book club, and they'd found a shared enthusiasm for a couple of writers. Now he was playing with Sam on the grass, the two of them engaged in a game of tag.

'Maybe he's got some to spare, not having a child to look after.'

'Hannah…' Her mother shot her a reproving look. 'You know I'll always look after Sam whenever you want.'

'I know. I didn't mean it like that, Mum. My time with Sam's the best part of my day, I wouldn't give it up for anything.'

'You could. If you wanted to go out sometimes.' Her mother looked pointedly across at Matt. 'Matt seems very nice, maybe he'd take you somewhere.'

Hannah rolled her eyes, trying to make out that the idea hadn't occurred to her already, and been rejected. 'Don't you start. I've only just managed to get Sophie to shut up about it.'

'Yes, she said.' Clearly her mum and Sophie had been

comparing notes. 'I dare say Sophie's been suggesting something a little more…intimate than a visit to the cinema.'

Hannah chuckled. Mum knew that Sophie didn't mince her words. 'Yes, she has.'

'You don't need to jump in with both feet.' Her mother glanced across at Matt. 'Although… I wouldn't blame you if you did.'

'Mum!'

'What, I'm not supposed to think about things like sex? He's very attractive. And where do you suppose you and your sisters came from? Your father and I—'

'Mum, stop!' Hannah rolled over onto her back, closing her eyes. 'As far as I'm concerned, you found us under a gooseberry bush. I'm not going to even consider any alternatives.'

'Whatever.' Her mother gave a sigh. 'But I've got some experience of this, Hannah. When your father died, I thought that it was the end of my world too. Don't get me wrong, I miss him every day, and I'll always be grateful to you for helping me through that time. But I have a few more things I want to accomplish now, and you should too.'

'You think that Sam and my job aren't enough for me?'

'You always say they are. It doesn't mean that you can't have more.'

Thankfully, her mother didn't press the point. She called Sam back over, and Matt followed, throwing himself down onto the grass.

'Sam, have something to drink, it's very hot.' Her mother produced one of Sam's favourite toys from her bag. 'And you can show Matt your spaceship if you like. He doesn't want to go running around too much, he's got another challenge to do this afternoon.'

Matt shot her mother a grateful look, and turned his attention to Sam's demonstration of the spaceship's various features. He was nice with him, always including him in his conversation and listening to his opinions, giving them as much weight as if he were an adult. Sam was unable to put Matt's respect for him into words, but he felt it and liked Matt.

After half an hour, the contestants were called back and escorted to the same rooms they'd been in that morning. There was no wait this time, and Matt was taken straight out again, leaving Hannah to wonder what was in store for them. He reappeared ten minutes later, holding the same helmets they'd been wearing that morning.

'No! Not another one?'

'Well, thankfully this one *is* sitting down.' He handed Hannah's helmet to her, and she saw that it was fitted out with the same goggles that he'd had earlier. 'You get to drive an electric buggy.'

'Blindfold… They want me to operate a vehicle blindfold.'

Matt shrugged. 'That's okay, isn't it? You've got me to tell you which way to go. The course is laid out in the park, next to the hospital. I drive you over there, and then you take over.'

She wondered if he'd felt this way this morning. Blind and reliant on him. Matt was allowed to steer her out of the building and across the grass, and every touch was electric. All that stood between her and the ground.

He helped her into the buggy and they made the short trip over to the park. It was announced that the contestants would have ten minutes to familiarise themselves with the vehicles, and Hannah slid across into the driving seat. His hands guided hers to the steering wheel and once she was confident about being able to find the forward and reverse gears without too much fumbling around, he bent down, guiding her feet to the accelerator and footbrake pedals.

'I've got it. How do I start this thing?'

She felt his fingertips touch her hand, guiding it towards the starter keys. She twisted them, hearing a muted whine as the electric engine started up. A few tentative moves forward and then backwards again, and then she heard someone shouting an instruction.

'We're going to start in a minute.' She heard Matt's voice in the speaker fitted to her helmet. 'I can't touch you now...'

Hannah shivered. It sounded like an erotic promise, just his voice in the darkness and a shared purpose...

'What are the others doing?' This was a race, and Hannah tried to keep her mind off anything that she and Matt might do together in the darkness. 'I can't hear their buggies.'

'No, everyone has their own separate course. Ours goes to the left of the ornamental pond and it looks as if the others go to the right.'

'Right. So when in doubt steer left, or we both end up in the water.'

His deep, low chuckle sounded in her ear. 'Yep. If we do, just hold onto the buggy and I'll fish you out. There's a slalom for starters, so go slowly. After that there's a straight run and you can speed up a bit.'

'Okay. Got it.' The fantasy of Matt in the darkness was replaced with one of Matt in the water, saving her. Hannah gripped the steering wheel tightly, waiting for the starting buzzer.

They made it through the slalom, Matt's voice in her ear encouraging her and telling her which way to steer. Then he told her to put her foot down and go a little faster.

'Stop!' His voice sounded in the microphone, suddenly tense. 'Hannah take the helmet off!'

That meant instant disqualification, they'd been told that. But Matt could see what was happening around them and she couldn't. Hannah pulled the helmet off, blinking in the sunlight. Matt already had the door of the buggy open, and he glanced back at her.

'This is real...'

CHAPTER EIGHT

THE SPECTATORS WERE ahead of them, in an area where the four courses converged at the finish line. Matt concentrated hard on directing Hannah, looking out for any obstacles in their path that the vehicle couldn't manage. He'd seen the young man fiddling with the bundle of power cables that ran beside the white lines on the grass that marked their route.

Something about the way he was yanking the cables, not seeming to know quite what he was doing, seemed wrong, and at odds with the usual professionalism of the camera crews. A sixth sense made Matt glance at the man a second time, and it was then that it happened. A spark, a cry and the man was thrown backwards. They were far enough away from the finish line and the other three teams that no one seemed to notice.

In the flood of adrenalin it didn't occur to him that this might be some carefully constructed feint to test them. This had all the awkward unpredictability of reality, and he was out of the vehicle before it had properly stopped, calling to Hannah. He ran across the grass, kneeling down beside the man.

He was pale, his lips blue. A burn on his arm where he'd touched the cable, and when Matt tore his shirt open and bent down to listen for a heartbeat, there was nothing.

Hannah was behind him somewhere and when he turned he saw her running towards them.

'Stay away from those cables! One of them may be damaged.' She swerved suddenly, giving the dark coil snaking through the grass a wide berth.

'Okay, I'll get them to switch the power off before anyone else gets hurt.' The van that held the camera crew, who'd been filming their progress, had stopped and Hannah hurried towards them.

Matt quickly checked the man's pulse again. A few thready irregular beats, which stopped again under his fingers. He positioned his hands carefully on the man's chest.

He'd done this many times before. Not here, under the heat of the afternoon sun, with a hundred different variables, one of which was a live electric cable, situated right behind him. Hannah was dealing with that… Matt forgot everything else, and started CPR.

Death could happen so quickly. And life equally quickly. As Hannah reached him, kneeling down on the other side of the man's prone body, Matt heard a rasping breath. He checked the man's pulse, and felt the regular beat of a heart that had responded to the rhythm of the chest compressions.

'Got him…' He murmured the words and Hannah nodded. The man's lips were rapidly regaining their pink colour, and his eyelids were fluttering, as if struggling to open.

She nodded. 'The camera crew have radioed down for a crash team from the hospital. They'll be here soon.'

People were running towards them now, and he heard someone shout at them to stay back. As the man's eyes opened, Hannah was there, taking hold of his hand, positioning herself so that her shadow fell across his face.

'You took a bit of a jolt there.' She smiled down at him. 'Just be still for a moment. The doctor has everything under control.'

The man nodded weakly. He still needed care, he had burns and the CPR would undoubtedly have bruised his ribs badly. But his pulse was beating under Matt's fingers. Hannah was checking the burns on his hand, and then she carefully took off his trainers, inspecting his feet.

'Not too bad. He must have been thrown clear.'

Matt realised suddenly that she hadn't seen what had happened. Hannah had reacted so quickly to the situation that he'd forgotten that.

'Yes, he was.'

By the time the medical team arrived, they'd ascertained all of the young man's injuries. Minor burns that were immediately wrapped with cool packs. There was a bump on the back of his head, and Matt borrowed a penlight to check his responses before he was loaded onto a stretcher to be ferried down to the hospital.

Hannah sat back on her heels, watching them go. Matt recognised her smile. It was the one that someone who knew they'd made a difference wore.

Then she turned, shading her eyes as she gazed towards the finish line. The yellows had already completed the course, and were celebrating their win, while the blues and greens fought it out for second place.

'I'm glad Laura and Jack made it this time. They had bad luck this morning.' Hannah turned the corners of her mouth down.

'Yeah. They deserve it.' Matt had made the only decision possible, but all decisions had a price. 'I'm…sorry.'

'What, that you forgot all about a stupid game and decided to go and save a man's life?' She shot him a reproving look.

She must feel it. Winning meant so much to Hannah. But she was the same as him, first and foremost a healer. Matt sighed, trying to make sense of his own feelings.

'We got to him quickly, and I think he'll be okay. That's more important than anything, but I think it's okay to wish that it hadn't happened. I imagine he does too.'

She nodded, tears suddenly forming in her eyes. 'Yeah. Let's not talk about that right now, eh?'

They sat for a moment in the sunshine. The generator had been turned off, and technicians were checking cables and coiling the damaged one. The director of the unit walked towards them.

'Nasty business.' He sat down on the grass. 'I'm glad you were there.'

'Me too.' Hannah was making an effort to smile.

'I…um…don't know what we can do about this. In terms of the competition… We want to make this fair.' The director seemed intent on catching Hannah's gaze, and she seemed intent on not looking at him.

'Give us a minute, will you?' Matt spoke firmly. 'Hannah needs to go and see her son, he'll be wondering what happened. I'd like to check on the man who was hurt, and make sure that he's all right before we do anything else.'

'Yes. Yes, of course. Thank you for what you did just now.'

Hannah smiled suddenly and got to her feet. 'It's all in a day's work.'

Matt had seen Hannah jogging over to where Sam and her mother were standing. No victory dance this time, but there was a hug. *That* was what really mattered.

He walked out of the park and onto the hospital grounds, finding his way to A and E. One of the doctors there told him that Joe, the young man who had been injured, was doing well and he allowed Matt to spend a few minutes with him.

Deep in thought as he left A and E and walked back towards the park, he almost bumped into Hannah.

'Hey! What's up, everything all right?' She looked a little down in the mouth.

'Yes, fine. How is he?'

'He's okay, recovering nicely. The burns aren't too bad, and he's conscious and talking.'

'That's great.'

'So what *is* up?' Hannah shrugged and Matt shook his head.

'Don't tell me nothing…'

She puffed out a breath. 'Everyone's being so nice. Jack and Laura came to find me, and said we should take first place. But they really deserve it, they came back after what happened this morning and they're set to win today. The director said that we could do the course again but…'

'That wouldn't be fair either. You've seen it now, and you're bound to do better.'

'Yes. Exactly.' She looked up at him, her expression troubled. 'I… This just doesn't feel right, Matt. We did what we did, and that's its own reward.'

Matt thought for a moment. 'I guess we've both given up a bit to do the jobs we do. You and Sophie catch an extra shift, and you can't get back home in time to put Sam to bed.' He couldn't think of anything that he was missing by working long hours. He'd made a point of not having any home life. But Hannah smiled, and nodded.

'So what do you say we let this result stand. We're disqualified because I made a decision to tell you to take your helmet off. We made the same decision that we've had to make all of our working lives. Let's stick by that, and be proud of it.'

'That's exactly how I feel about it. But… It's not just us. What will the hospital board say if we pass up the chance of winning the money?' Hannah frowned.

'It's a matter of principle. If they have anything to say about it, then we have our answer. We can still win if we make a good showing on the final day.'

He wanted to tell her that if they didn't win, he'd help her raise the money for the hospital anyway. But he might not even be here in a couple of months. His application for the job in London was under consideration, and he'd been called for an interview.

They'd come a long way in the last three weeks. Complete strangers, who'd treated each other with prickly courtesy but didn't really trust each other. But now Matt knew her. And he knew what Hannah would choose to do.

She looked up at him, the sunlight catching flecks of gold in her eyes. 'You're right. I say we disqualify ourselves from the race. We did the right thing, and we don't need any rewards for that. Thank you, Matt.'

Suddenly he needed her close. Winning together was nothing if they couldn't lose together as well. Matt reached for her, and Hannah smiled up at him.

'I'm okay...'

'Not sure that I am.'

She wrinkled her nose. 'Maybe I spoke too soon.'

She put her arms around him, and Matt held her close. None of the people milling around seemed to notice, they were just teammates hugging each other. But this was different. It was everything. Sharing the disasters along with the triumphs, and knowing that Hannah was there with him.

'We should go.' She didn't move.

'Yeah, we should. In a moment.'

He felt her move against him, snuggling into his arms. Matt held his breath, wanting this to last. 'Yeah. In a moment...'

The announcement of the winners took place a little later than expected, but most of the spectators were still there. Pretty much everyone knew what had happened, and wanted to know how things would be resolved.

Matt had had a lengthy conversation with the head judge, and when she approached the microphone, she held a piece of paper in her hand. Clearly what she was about to say had been carefully scripted.

She started by giving the news that the young man who had been injured was doing well. Then she praised each of the teams for their performances today. Suddenly she looked up from her notes, staring straight into the camera.

'I've mentored medical staff in training for many years, and today I saw a fine example of the values that we teach. Hannah and Matt have asked that the results of this afternoon's heat stand, as a tribute to the many medical professionals around the country who put their own interests second and respond to a higher calling on a daily basis. So, after a brave comeback, I'm happy to award the medals to Laura and Jack of the yellow team. Ladies and gentlemen, you are all winners.'

There was a moment's silence. Then a piercing whistle sounded from the crowd. 'Go, Laura and Jack… Go, Hannah and Matt.' Sophie was shouting at the top of her voice, and as everyone else took up the chant, she and Sam performed the victory dance.

'Your words?' Hannah nudged Matt, whispering up to him.

'I just explained how we felt. I thought she put it very well…'

Before they could say any more, Laura and Jack had come over to shake their hands. Then the others, and before Hannah knew what was happening, she was being propelled forward. Laura and Jack beckoned to the others, and all eight of the competitors stood at the front of the stage together, waving at the crowd.

Hannah felt tears tumbling down her cheeks. She wanted to share this with Matt, but he was further down the line of competitors. She waved at Sam, and he waved back, obviously shouting at the top of his voice, although the sound was lost in all the cheering.

By the time she managed to escape and walk down the steps of the stage, Hannah's legs were shaking. She wanted to cling to Matt and hear him tell her that they were in this together, Flash and Robin, teammates…and maybe more? She shook the thought out of her head as the chairman of the hospital board hurried across to her.

'I know you're disappointed, Hannah. But you showed a very fine example today.' He took her hand, shaking it vigorously.

'Thank you.' This was the first time that Dr Gregson had even spoken to her, and she couldn't think of anything else to say.

'This is your little boy…?' Dr Gregson gestured towards where Sophie and Sam were hovering, Sophie holding onto Sam's hand to stop him running forward.

'Yes. Sam… And my ambulance partner, Sophie Turner.'

'Sam…' Dr Gregson bent down, smiling, and Sam looked up at him with the clear-eyed look of someone who had no inkling of hospital hierarchies. 'You must be very proud of your mum.'

'She's the best. Do you want to see our victory dance?' Sam flung his arms above his head, ready to start doing the victory dance again, and Sophie grabbed hold of him. Dr Gregson laughed.

'I'll leave you to your celebrations.' He glanced down at Sam again. 'Keep doing that victory dance, young man.' Dr Gregson turned, making a beeline for Matt and shaking his hand.

'That went well.' Sophie was staring after him.

'Yes, I'm glad he understood.'

Sophie nodded. Matt had extricated himself from Dr Gregson's grip and was walking towards them, smiling.

'Hey, Sam. How's your day been?'

'We won!' Sam probably didn't understand quite how or why they'd won, just that they had.

'That's right. Go, reds…'

Sam reached up towards Matt in an unmistakable gesture. Matt hesitated for a moment and then picked the boy up, settling him onto his shoulders. His obvious affection for her son was always accompanied by a slight awkwardness.

'I've got to go in a minute.' Sophie looked at her watch. 'Got a date with the new A and E doctor. He's intrigued by my parking.'

Matt chuckled. 'Obviously a man of great insight.'

'So what about you two losers?' Sophie grinned. 'Off to celebrate?'

'Enough of the losers. We can still win.' Hannah saw Matt's jaw set in a determined line.

'It would be very close...' She shrugged.

'If we win outright next week, we'll be one point ahead of the others. So that's exactly what we're going to do.' A hint of steel showed in his blue eyes. Suddenly Hannah didn't want his comfort any more. *This* was exactly what she wanted from Matt.

'Okay, then. That's what we'll do.'

Sophie chuckled. 'That's the spirit. I'll leave you to plot your strategies, I've got to run...'

She grinned up at Sam, pointing towards her cheek in a signal that this was where she wanted a goodbye kiss. Sam leaned down towards her, and Sophie stood on her toes, hanging onto Matt as she did so. So easy, so natural. Hannah supposed that it was because Sophie didn't feel the way that she did about him. Sophie could touch Matt without feeling any melting desire to fall into his arms.

'What do you have planned for tonight?' Matt started to walk towards the car park, and Hannah fell into step beside him.

'Mum's out for dinner with her book club, so it's going to be just the two of us and a cartoon marathon.'

He frowned. 'Shame. I was hoping that you might let me return last week's favour and buy you dinner. But a cartoon marathon's a tough thing to compete with.'

He could come home with them... The offer hovered on the tip of her tongue, but Hannah's courage failed her. If

Sam could be persuaded to go to bed on time, then she'd be alone with Matt.

'There's a great place on the river. Family friendly…'

This was why she shouldn't be alone with him. He was just too tempting for words. But what could happen under the watchful eye of a six-year-old boy?

'Thank you. We'd really like that, wouldn't we, Sam?'

'Yes, okay.' Sam hardly glanced at her, obviously bound up in his own thoughts and oblivious of what he'd just agreed to.

'Great. I'll come and pick you up at six.'

'You look bee-yoo-tiful!' Sam elongated the word to give it particular emphasis.

Hannah had only washed her hair and grabbed a dress from the wardrobe. And applied a little make-up. And found her favourite sandals, which matched the blue of her dress perfectly.

There was no point in protesting to Sam, he hadn't developed the skill of discernment yet. 'Well, you look beautiful too.' Sam frowned and Hannah laughed. 'Okay, you don't look beautiful at all. You look handsome and *very* cool.'

'Thank you.' Sam was wearing his best jeans and trainers, with a stripy polo shirt and a hoodie. When Hannah had tried to comb his hair he'd wriggled and protested, running his hands through it so that it stood on end. Hannah had relented, wetting the comb and making the spikes a little more regular.

Her beautiful boy. She was so proud of him, and if she wanted to admire anyone tonight, Sam was a good choice. That resolution flew straight out of the window as soon as the doorbell rang and she opened the door.

Matt was wearing an off-white linen suit, just creased enough to appear relaxed. A crisp, dark blue shirt completed the look. No… *Matt* completed the look. Blond and tanned, his eyes seeming very blue and his shoulders very broad. He was simply mouth-watering.

'You look nice.' The curve of his lips told her that he considered this an understatement.

'She looks bee-yoo-tiful,' Sam corrected him, and Matt nodded solemnly in agreement.

Hannah laughed, trying to cover her embarrassment. 'Sam's gone for cool tonight.'

'Hmm.' Matt pressed his lips together. 'So did I but I think you've managed it a lot better than I did, Sam.'

'You look okay. Are we going in *your* car?' Sam craned around him, obviously interested in the sleek, dark blue car parked outside. Hannah had to admit that it was far more likely to appeal to Sam than her own red run-around.

'If your mum doesn't mind me borrowing your car seat.' Matt shot a querying glance at Hannah and she shook her head.

'No, that's fine. Mine's easy to swap over into different cars, Sophie doesn't have one either so we're always switching it.'

She transferred the car seat into Matt's car, careful not to scratch the leather upholstery, and Sam sat quietly as they drove, transfixed by the dashboard display. They meandered through country lanes, drawing up next to a quiet, tree-lined stretch of the River Colne.

'A boat!' Sam was wide-eyed with excitement, and Matt smiled.

They walked down the gangplank onto a red and white painted barge, which had been fitted out with bench seats and tables. The evening sun sparkled on the water, and they sat under the shade of a canvas awning.

Matt was the perfect host, making sure that they both had whatever they wanted. The waiters were attentive and friendly, bringing a glass of wine for Hannah and sparkling water for Matt and Sam. Sam responded to being treated like an adult by acting like one, and her little boy suddenly seemed very grown up.

'Mum, look. Swans…' Sam knelt on his seat, hanging over the side of the boat, and Hannah grabbed hold of him before he fell overboard. He twisted round, taking a bread roll from the basket on the table.

'No, we mustn't give them bread, Sam. It's not what they're meant to eat, and it isn't good for them.'

Sam slid back into his seat and Matt pushed his plate towards him. 'You can give them some lettuce.' He started to separate the shredded lettuce from his mixed salad with his fork.

'Lettuce?' Hannah raised her eyebrows. 'Really?'

'Yes, swans like lettuce, and it doesn't do them any harm. A bit like pondweed, I suppose.'

Sam picked up the lettuce, and Hannah grabbed hold of him again as he climbed up, leaning over the side of the boat. When he scattered the lettuce on the water, the swans dipped their long necks, gobbling it up.

'They're making a funny noise…' Sam shivered with laughter, and Hannah saw Matt gesture to one of the waiters. He disappeared, coming back with a small bowl of shredded lettuce. Matt was grinning broadly, enjoying this as much as Sam was.

This was so relaxing. So nice. Taking the world as it came, on a lazy river, as the sun began to go down. If she'd been with Sam's father…

There wouldn't have been times like these. Sam was John's son, but Matt was the one who had time for him. And whatever she'd seen in John felt like a pale counterfeit of the way she was beginning to feel about Matt. She knew that Sam would benefit from having a father figure in his life, but this was the first time she'd wanted someone for herself in a very long time.

They lingered over coffee, talking. The lights that were threaded around the canvas awning began to brighten in the gathering dusk, and Matt signalled to the waiter to bring the bill.

'Thank you so much for tonight, Matt.' Hannah turned to him as they stepped off the gangplank and onto the path that led up to the car. 'It was just what I needed after today.'

'Me too. Thank you for coming.' He reached out suddenly, brushing her arm with his fingertips. The world around her began to melt away, shrivelling in the heat of his gaze, as somehow the impossible didn't seem quite so impossible after all. Unspoken words hung in the air between them, waiting impatiently for the chance to be turned into reality.

Then, from somewhere behind her, Hannah heard Sam's thin wail of distress. He'd found his way down to the water's edge, and one of the swans that he'd been feeding had left the water and was waddling towards him. Sam was standing quite still, transfixed by the lumbering creature that was more than twice his size.

Before she could move, Matt was there. He gathered Sam up in his arms, shooing the swan away from him. When he turned back towards Hannah, his jaw was set hard in a mask of distress.

'Hey, little man. You're all right...' He was trying to smile for Sam's sake, and not making a very good job of it. Sam was crying now, and the agony on Matt's face as he strode back to where Hannah was standing was obvious.

They'd been close by, and Hannah had only taken her eyes off Sam for one moment. That moment had been enough, though, and the unforgivable part of it all was that Hannah's eyes had been on Matt. All of her attention had been on Matt, and she'd let Sam wander off.

She swallowed hard, trying to control her panic. This wasn't the same as leaving her family and following John halfway around the world. She hadn't abandoned Sam in favour of Matt. All the same, when Matt delivered Sam into her arms, she hugged her son as tightly as she could.

'Mum… Mum, you're squeezing me.' Sam's tears had disappeared as abruptly as they'd appeared, and he was wiping his nose on the shoulder of her best dress. Still holding onto her son, Hannah managed to swipe her own tears away before either Matt or Sam could notice them.

'I'm sorry, sweetie. The swans are pretty big close up, aren't they?'

Sam nodded. 'I think it *might* have eaten me. But it didn't.'

'No, of course it didn't. Swans don't eat little boys, they eat lettuce. We just have to make sure that we stay away from them when they get out of the water. If they get frightened and flap their wings, they could hurt us.' Hannah managed a smile and Sam cheered up immediately, eyeing the swan as it drifted serenely at the water's edge.

'How *big* are they when they flap their wings?' Now that he was safe in her arms, he was clearly thinking about the logistics of the matter. 'Not as big as Matt.'

'No, not as big as Matt.'

'That's all right, then.' Sam had assessed the situation with a child's logic, and decided that Matt's presence made everything all right. It was a very tempting conclusion to make, and Hannah resisted it.

Sam's assertion didn't seem to be convincing Matt either. He still seemed distressed about the incident. But he smiled, taking his car keys from his pocket.

'Would you like to try out the computer in my car?' He'd obviously seen Sam's interest in the dashboard, and seemed to be trying his best to make things up to Sam. The little boy slithered down from her arms, running to Matt.

'Yes!'

'You've done it now. We'll be here all evening while he switches things on and off.'

Matt didn't seem to mind that. He didn't mind fingermarks on the high-tech touchscreen controls either. In the end, Hannah called a halt to the endless questions, and Sam was strapped firmly into his car seat for the drive home.

The house was still dark, and Hannah let Sam run past her into the sitting room. 'Would you like to come in for some coffee?' The words flew recklessly from her lips, and when he shook his head it was almost a relief.

'Thanks, but you probably need to get Sam to bed now.'

'Yes, any minute now he's going to realise that he's tired and keel over.'

Matt nodded. 'I'd best get going. I'll see you next week.'

She couldn't turn away from him. She needed him to touch her, just once, before she let him go. Hannah reprimanded herself. Had she forgotten already what had happened the last time she'd gazed at Matt, her attention only on him and not on what Sam had been doing?

A thump from the sitting room settled the question.

'I'd better go and see what he's up to. Goodnight, Matt. And thank you.'

'Thank *you*. I really enjoyed tonight.' For one moment, the heat of his gaze seemed like the touch of a lover. Then he turned quickly, walking to his car.

CHAPTER NINE

MATT HAD BEEN thinking about the swan all week. He'd rationalised it. The beautiful creature, gliding over the water with barely a ripple in its wake, had turned so quickly into a lumbering, terrifying threat. It was all about his internal child, and how his father's moods had turned on a whisper into something dark and dangerous.

But he still couldn't get the picture of Sam, standing paralysed by fear, out of his head. The boy had recovered quickly, but it had shaken Matt to the core.

He wanted so much to love Hannah. He was rapidly beginning to care for Sam as well, and Matt wanted to protect the boy. But he'd been taught a valuable lesson, which he should heed. Love had its responsibilities, and it would be better never to love than to fail the people he cared about.

But today he didn't need to fall in love with her. He just needed to win. *They* needed to tap into the connection they'd made and win.

His senses had become attuned to the sight of the red T-shirt. It was a precursor of all the other delights, her scent and her smile, and when he caught sight of it he couldn't help a thrill of anticipation.

'Hey, Flash…' He walked up behind her, murmuring the words, as she stood alone looking at the large marquee that had been erected in the grounds of the fourth hospital.

She whirled around, reddening a little, as if he'd caught her thinking something she shouldn't.

'Hey. Are you ready, Robin?'

'One hundred percent.' More, if that were possible. If wanting to do anything for your partner counted, then they'd win by a mile.

'Sorry. I've only got ninety-nine…'

He grinned. 'That'll do.'

'I hope so.' She turned the corners of her mouth down. 'I'm still having a little trouble with my knee. Not so you'd notice, but I get a few twinges when I run.'

That was new. Hannah wasn't just admitting a weakness, she was asking for his help and encouragement. It was a surprising start to the day.

If he needed to, he'd pick her up and carry her across whatever finish line lay ahead of them. The thought was unexpectedly sweet. But if wanting your teammate so badly that he thought it would crush him at times was an unorthodox incentive, he'd take it. Whatever it took to win.

'I can run for both of us. Anyway, they'll have to ring the changes at some point and concentrate on our medical skills, so hopefully there won't *be* too much running.'

'Yeah. We'll be okay.' She gave him a smile that reverberated through his whole being.

For the first time, all of the contestants were gathered together to hear their challenge for the day. A succession of medical problems that had been devised to test their skills under pressure. The marquee was divided up into four consulting areas, each with a camera and a judge in attendance.

'Thank goodness.' Hannah walked towards the red team's compartment, and Matt saw a little stiffness in the way that she moved. Ninety-nine percent had been an exaggeration—he calculated that she was only eighty percent fit.

They had ten minutes to arrange their workspace. A temporary floor was laid, and the cubicle was furnished with an examination couch and a desk, two chairs on either side of it.

'What do you say we get rid of this?' Matt gestured towards the desk.

'Good idea.'

He pulled the desk back, grouping the four chairs in front of it. Hannah nodded her approval.

'That's better. Nothing to separate us from our patients.'

'Right. Are we all set?'

'Just about.' Hannah pulled the phone over to the other side of the desk, so that it was in reach, and picked up the thick pad of paper. 'You talk and I'll write?'

She was deferring to his status as a senior doctor. Matt didn't have a lot of time for that, Hannah's experience was different but no less valuable. 'We'll take turns.'

The challenge started in earnest, and their patients came thick and fast. In the few moments he could spare to think about anything other than the problem before him, Matt was impressed with the way that their obviously healthy patients had been schooled in exactly what symptoms they should be showing, and made up to give all of the appearance of having various complaints. There were a few very minor injuries, one of which concealed a greater problem. Hannah had a way of quickly spotting the difference between a teenager who just required a plaster on his finger and a woman whose black eye was as a result of difficulties with her balance.

Matt found a case of unregulated diabetes, and called for emergency support. When a man appeared with a well-designed glove over his hand and arm, made of practice suture skin, which had been slashed to imitate a deep cut, Hannah smilingly moved to one side while he stitched it. As the man left, a bell rang and the judge, who had been sitting silently in the corner, told them that they had a thirty-minute break.

'Good thing we have a surgeon on the team. I learned

something.' Hannah was making for the exit of the mar-quee and Matt followed her.

'Where are we going?'

'Canteen. That's my area of expertise, I know where the canteen and the washrooms are in every hospital in the district. Sophie and I sometimes end up here with patients for the specialist burns unit.'

'I think I must be getting soft...' It was a long time since he'd seen so many different people in just three hours, and it looked as if there would be more this afternoon.

Hannah's assessing glance almost made him blush. Matt hadn't realised he'd retained that ability. Today was turn-ing into a walk down memory lane, in more ways than one.

'No. You're not getting soft.'

Coffee, protein and calories. Matt hadn't lost the knack of pacing himself, and eating for staying power. He added two bottles of water and a couple of energy bars to his tray, and they took them with them when they hurried back to the marquee.

He was a delight to watch. Confident and yet always on the lookout to make sure there was nothing he'd missed. Hannah had learned a few things from him during the course of the morning, and yet he was always happy to stand back and let her work when her own knowledge and skills were most useful to them.

They were a dream team. Very different but able to work together. If they didn't win today, it wouldn't be for want of trying, and certainly not through any lack of expertise. Matt's specialty might be surgery, but he had an encyclo-paedic knowledge of many other aspects of medicine.

Whatever happened, they could hold their heads high in the knowledge that they'd given this their best shot. They could go back to their jobs on Monday...

Hannah tried to ignore the sinking feeling in the pit of her stomach. She loved her job, but it didn't bring her into contact with Matt on a daily basis. Losing him seemed suddenly worse than losing their chance at the prize for their hospital.

They worked until they were both exhausted. Another three hours, and then a half-hour break before a final three hours. When the judge told them that they were finished, she flopped into her chair, puffing out a sigh.

'Whatever happens...' Matt sat down, catching her gaze. Those blue eyes were always like a sensual tide, washing over her.

'Whatever happens, we gave it our best shot. Thank you so much, Matt.'

'It's been a privilege.'

The feeling of wanting to reach for him was tearing her apart and he seemed to understand that. He glanced up at the cameras mounted around the edges of the compartment, quirking his lips down. The touch of his long fingers, moving slightly on the arm of his seat, seemed designed only for her.

That was all there was. Something unspoken. The heat of his gaze and the sudden and certain knowledge that he felt something too. Something that neither of them could act upon.

'How long do you think it'll be?' Two minutes of this was delicious. Any more and the longing for what she couldn't have would turn to torture.

'She said half an hour. And I know just how to spend it...'

Here? In front of the cameras? Hannah dragged her imagination away from the only thing that she could think of right now, the caress of his lips on hers. He couldn't possibly mean that...

'How's that?'

'Get on the couch.' Her eyebrows shot up and Matt grinned, as if he knew exactly what she'd been thinking.

'I'd like to take a look at your knee. Assuming it's not okay, that is.'

Hannah grinned. 'Of course it's okay, what else did you expect? I'll humour you, though.'

'Thank you. I'd appreciate it.'

She sat on the edge of the couch, swinging her feet. Matt nodded towards the leg of her sweatpants, and Hannah rolled it up, taking off the support he'd given her last week.

He flexed her leg up and down, his fingers resting lightly on the side of her knee, on just the spot that it hurt. 'There's still some inflammation there.'

'I haven't had much chance to rest it. But even if we do win, it's two weeks before the finals.'

'Yeah. You know what to do, keep going with the ice, and try to stay off it as much as you can. If it gets any worse then you might need a short course of anti-inflammatories.'

Hannah nodded, wrapping the support back around her knee and getting to her feet. A sharp stab of pain told her that she'd got it wrong and the support needed some adjustment.

'Let me…' He bent down and suddenly his gaze met hers. The now familiar chemistry started to fizzle between them, and Hannah jerked backwards.

'No, I'll do it.' She willed him to understand what she didn't say.

Not in front of the cameras.

He nodded. Neither of them could deny it any more, but that was between the two of them. They could hide it from everyone else.

They walked companionably out of the tent, wandering down to greet Sam and her mother. Everything as it should be. The light in his eyes had been quenched, and Matt was just a teammate again.

The wait wasn't so bad. Hannah concentrated on Sam, and going to get ice cream for everyone took up a few minutes. Then they were called to the stage to hear the judges' verdict.

If Matt felt anything, then he was hiding it well. He smiled at the other competitors, seeming more relaxed than anyone as they chatted together. The challenges had brought all eight of them together, and whoever went on to the finals would do so with the blessing of the others.

There was the usual preamble...thanking everyone for being here, praising each of the teams and giving everyone a special mention. Then the verdict.

'This has been more than just a competition. We've seen all our teams hold true to their values and exhibit bravery and determination. Our winners today will be going forward to represent Hertfordshire in the finals, and we wish them well in the challenges to come. Ladies and gentlemen... Matt and Hannah!'

There was a roar of applause that seemed to come from somewhere very far away. Hannah hardly heard the congratulations from the other teams, and barely felt the hands that shook hers.

'Matt...?'

He was there. The only thing that was real. Matt grinned at her, hugging her in the kind of bear hug that a teammate might give. They'd done it. Despite everything, they'd really done it.

She received her medal, and then turned back, beckoning to the others to come forward. This moment was for everyone. The roar of the crowd increased as all eight of the competitors joined them, waving to the crowd.

It was surreal. She had what she'd wanted, and now she couldn't see any way forward from here. She *had* to talk to Matt, somewhere alone.

Something was up. Matt could see it in Hannah's demeanour, and feel it, nagging away in his own chest. There were issues, ones of their own making, and they both knew it.

It wouldn't have mattered so much if they'd lost. They could have bowed out gracefully, congratulating the winners and knowing they'd given it their best shot. Hannah would have disappeared back into her world, and he could have gone back to his. Whether or not he got the job down in London, he'd be gone soon. Matt knew that there would be other opportunities, and that his decision that it was about time he moved on was the driving factor in making those opportunities into a reality.

'Would you like to pop back to mine for a quick coffee? It's on your way home, and maybe we can plan our next move.' His offer was deliberately casual, as if this was just a matter of teammates sitting down together for half an hour to talk. But those moments alone with her in the tent had persuaded him that they *did* need to talk and that the conversation might not be an easy one.

'That's a good idea.' She glanced back towards Sam and her mother. 'I'll just let Mum know that I'll be back home later.'

He nodded. He knew what would come next. Watching while Sam and Hannah performed the victory dance, and Hannah draped her medal around her son's neck. He'd seen them do it before, but it never ceased to delight him, and he stared at them, hungry for every moment of the little ceremony.

He gave her the address, and saw her car following his through the Saturday evening traffic, back to the flat close to the hospital that he'd occupied for the last year. When Hannah parked behind him, and he led the way upstairs to his front door, it seemed that he'd merely occupied it. It wasn't a home, the way her house was.

'This is nice.' She looked around when he ushered her into the sitting room. Tidy and impersonal, all of the furniture selected by the landlord. It was pretty much the same as the day he'd walked in here, apart from the clothes in the wardrobe and the two boxes of his most valued possessions that were stored in the cupboard in the hallway.

'It's…close to the hospital.' The large windows gave a great view of the centre of the town, and the hospital was within walking distance.

'It has loads of potential.'

Yeah. Potential. There wasn't much point in realising that potential, because he'd always known that he'd be moving on. Having to tear yourself away from a place that he'd made into a home wasn't something that Matt ever reckoned on doing.

'I just wanted to talk.' Now that they were here, he didn't know how to put it into words. The situation was clear enough, the irresistible attraction that they'd found together was real, but it wasn't something that he could act on. Putting that tactfully and yet clearly was his problem.

'Yes, I know.' She turned her gaze on him and he was trapped again. In one of those delicious moments that he fought to ignore, but didn't know how. 'Where's that coffee you promised me?'

That was a much easier prospect. She followed him into the kitchen, looking around at the shiny white cupboard doors, and sleek stainless-steel fittings.

'Wow. Do you ever cook in here, or just make coffee.'

'I cook.' He opened the refrigerator door, and the contents betrayed him. Two pints of milk, four large cartons of juice and a ready meal. He grabbed some milk, and closed the door again quickly. This had suddenly turned into an exercise in questioning his lifestyle, and Matt was happy with the way he lived. No ties that could turn into bonds. No strings to cut.

She leaned back against the worktop, watching him, as he filled the machine with water and ground coffee. Then Hannah spoke.

'Matt, this has been hard for us both. Making the kind

of relationship that allows us to push our own boundaries, and win.'

That was a good start. Matt wished he'd thought of it himself. 'I think we've done pretty well.'

'Yes, we have. This next phase is going to be even more challenging.' She gave him a knowing look.

Coffee had dripped into the two cups, and he added milk to Hannah's, leaving his black. He could do with the bite, to concentrate his thoughts. She walked across the room, picking up her cup, and then retreated back to the other side of the kitchen.

'Hannah, over the last four weeks I've come to really respect you. You're an amazing person.' An amazing *woman*. But it was best not to think of their partnership as that of a man and a woman.

She took a sip from her cup, as if allowing his words to sink in. 'That's nice. Thank you.'

'If I were anyone else, I'd... I wouldn't be hesitating. Last week, I wouldn't have let you turn away from me on the doorstep, without asking if I might kiss you.' He gave a smiling shrug. 'I would have followed up with roses, of course.'

'It sounds as if I've been missing out.' She was tracing the rim of her cup with her finger. 'You're not... I don't know. You don't have a secret wife or girlfriend somewhere, do you?'

'No, I've never been married, and I don't have a significant other either. It's nothing like that.'

'Then you could be in witness protection.' She was regarding him steadily. 'Or you could have a dark past...'

'No.' She was getting warmer, and Matt would prefer that Hannah stop there. 'Nothing like that either. Just... baggage.'

She narrowed her eyes in thought. 'I know about baggage. So what kind of baggage makes you ask me out for a meal and then change your mind when you get to my doorstep? Don't get me wrong, I'm not blaming you for it, I haven't been all that consistent either.'

Hannah was refreshingly honest. And she made it sound as if she'd hear pretty much anything that he could say, and understand. He liked that about her.

'I didn't have much of a childhood. My work is everything and settling down with someone—anyone—just isn't for me. But I do care about you, and that's why I've been giving you the kind of mixed signals that don't produce very good teamwork.'

She nodded. 'If I hadn't waited for you to ask, and kissed you...?'

The thought made him tremble. Locked in Hannah's gaze, he couldn't dismiss it as just something that would have rounded the evening off nicely.

'I would have loved every minute of it.'

'Every *minute*?'

It was useless to suppose that if Hannah had kissed him, it wouldn't have lasted minutes. The flush of her cheeks showed Matt that she knew that as well as he did. He could have kissed her for hours without quenching the impulse to kiss her again.

He had to think rationally, though. Matt tore his thoughts from all that their kisses might have meant to him.

'Can we just accept this, Hannah? That there's something between us, but neither of us wants to take it any further. Just let it be.'

She smiled. 'I guess...yes. I'd like that.'

'So we're good? Ready to face whatever's thrown at us next, and win this thing?'

'Yes, we're good. I really want to win too, and we needed to clear the air a little.'

The air between them didn't feel at all clear. It felt full of all the same heavy anticipation and frustrated longing that had built up over the last month. But they'd acknowledged what they both wanted out of this, and that would stand them in good stead for London, and the finals of *Hospital Challenge*.

Hannah drained her cup, putting it into the sink. 'I'd better be going. I think that Sam wants to do the victory dance. Yet again…'

That was his cue to let her go. Matt had every intention of letting her go, but he couldn't, not just yet. It wasn't helping that Hannah was suddenly still, her gaze locked with his. Matt had thought that acknowledging this would make it easier to set it aside…

Hannah took one step towards him. 'Since we both know exactly where we stand now, I'm just wondering whether our own victory dance would be out of the question?'

Actually… No, it wouldn't. There could be no harm in stepping across the boundaries now, since they both knew exactly what the boundaries were. It gave them permission for a little flirting.

'Not sure I can manage the wiggle…not the way you do it, anyway.' Matt allowed himself a step. They were standing close now.

'We could go for something a little more sensual.'

Matt reached for her, laying his hand lightly on her back. She curled her fingers into his other hand, and he felt her body against his. The effect was electrifying. He took a few slow dance steps, feeling her follow his movements.

'Like this?'

'It's a great start.' He felt Hannah's hand on his arm, and as the muscles flexed involuntarily under her touch, she smiled.

Breathless moments, locked in each other's arms. Matt knew that anyone with any sense of caution would move away now, but he couldn't. He ached for just one step further.

'I can't help wondering…' She laid her head against his shoulder. Matt knew exactly what she was wondering because he was wondering too.

But before he kissed her he had to hear her say it. Out loud and in words of one syllable. 'May I—'

'Yes, you may.' Suddenly, he was too impatient to let her even finish. Matt raised an eyebrow and she laughed. 'Kiss me. Then I can kiss you back…'

Maybe that would be an end to it. But he wanted this, even if he couldn't take any more from Hannah. He wanted to show her that if things had been different then he could have loved her.

She stood on her toes, and he bent, kissing her lips. Just as soft and sweet tasting as he'd imagined, but he hadn't bargained on the searing jolt of feeling that ran down his spine. Hannah's hand gripped his shoulder and she gasped as he lifted her up, turning round to sit her on the kitchen counter.

'Too much…?'

She grinned. 'Not enough.'

The more he let hunger percolate into his kiss, the better Hannah liked it. He planted his hands on the counter top, on either side of her, leaning forward as she wrapped her arms around his neck. It was sweet and arousing, and he was going to have to stop soon… Not just yet, though.

When he drew back, he found he was still caught in her gaze, and there wasn't one thing he could do about it. Hannah had to be the one to set him free.

'I really do have to go.'

'I know.' He stole one last kiss from her lips and then lifted her down onto her feet. Keeping his arms around her, he began a long, slow dance that took them out of the kitchen and into the hallway.

'I like this…' Hannah laughed and he performed a dip, holding her securely in his arms. His lips almost touched hers in another kiss but not quite. This had to end soon, but while it lasted he'd squeeze every ounce of delight from it.

He managed to get the front door open without breaking the swaying motion, and then Hannah spun away from him. He raised her fingers to his lips, in one last gesture.

'Goodnight, Hannah.' Her real name suited the moment a little better than the joking nicknames.

'Goodnight, Matt.' She gave him one last smile, and then she was gone. He heard her footsteps on the stairs that led down to the lobby and he closed the door, leaning back against it.

That should have been a big mistake. Something that led to an embarrassed goodbye and the need to make things right afterwards. But it wasn't. They'd struggled against this, but it was what they both wanted. Maybe making it clear that it was just for this moment, and it would lead nowhere, had made it all the sweeter.

And somehow it had made things easier. No more wondering what might happen if he kissed her. They had a way forward, and that way was clear. In two weeks' time it would lead to the greatest test they'd faced.

CHAPTER TEN

HE'D BEEN PERFECT. Kissing her as if she wasn't just the most beautiful woman in the world, she was the *only* woman. Dancing her slowly towards the door, and in a gesture of old-fashioned charm kissing her hand. Every time she thought about it, she was back in that moment, feeling everything she'd felt then.

The idea that any man could make her want him so badly should have been terrifying. But Matt understood that this would go nowhere, and so did she. They'd allowed it in because they both wanted it, but it wouldn't divert them from their purpose.

Texting him had been a lot easier than it had before. Hannah had asked herself none of the agonised questions about whether this was too soon, or not soon enough. When she'd received the email, giving details of their trip to London, she'd just picked up her phone and suggested they meet to discuss it.

Their arrangements to meet up for coffee, at the end of Hannah's shift, had been put off for a day. A major accident on the bypass around the town had left ten people, travelling on a coach, with serious injuries, and they were both busy. The next day, Hannah was waiting for him in the hospital canteen.

Matt sat down in the chair she'd saved for him, and

Hannah pushed towards him the black coffee she'd bought for him.

'You got this for me? Thanks.'

'I'm guessing you must be tired.' She could voice those concerns now that they'd come to an understanding. It was okay to feel something, and okay to notice him.

'Yeah. We were operating pretty late into the night last night.' He smiled suddenly. 'We didn't lose anyone.'

'Thanks. I was wondering, and Sophie and I haven't had a chance to find out yet.'

'There were a number of injuries that were as a result of passengers being thrown around in the coach that was hit. The driver was badly hurt, and he'll probably need more surgery, but he's stable and doing better than I'd expected.'

Hannah nodded. She didn't often get the opportunity to discuss the patients she brought in with the surgeon in charge of their case, and this was the kind of good news that both she and Sophie always hoped for.

'I was worried about him. He'd lost a lot of blood from his stomach wound.'

Matt nodded. 'You were right to be. There was a lot of damage, and we had to remove his spleen. But if my stitches hold, then he should be okay, given time.'

'They'll hold.' Hannah grinned at him. It was okay to recognise that Matt was a talented surgeon as well.

'I'm grateful for your confidence in me.' His gaze met hers, and Hannah didn't try to fight it. They'd acknowledged this, and set their boundaries.

'So. What about the email, then...?' She reached into her pocket for the paper copy she'd made, and found that Matt had a similar copy in his hand. They both smiled at the synchronicity.

'It seems pretty straightforward. Nothing about what we'll be doing, just that we need to turn up on Thursday evening, and we'll have no contact with the outside world until the winners are announced the following Monday evening.'

Hannah nodded. She hadn't explained yet to Sam that she wouldn't be calling him every day. 'That's the first hurdle…'

'I…um…took the liberty of calling them. I asked whether contestants might be allowed one call to their families every day, and they said yes. Supervised, of course, so that you don't get to chat about the competition. But you can call Sam and tell him goodnight.'

He'd done that for her. Matt clearly wasn't too worried about calling his family.

'Thank you. It didn't occur to me to do that, I just hated the idea of not being able to talk to him.'

'Yeah, I didn't much like the idea either.' He scanned the paper in front of him again. 'How are you getting down to London?'

'I thought the train?'

'I was going to take my car. The hotel has parking for guests, and you never know, we might need it.'

'Won't they provide us with cars if we need them?'

He shrugged. 'Who knows? It can't hurt to prepare for every eventuality. Would you like a lift down there?'

'Yes, okay. Thanks. What are you taking in the way of…anything else?'

'A full range of clothes. From a smart suit to sweats and trainers.'

That sounded a bit over the top. They weren't going for a whole month. But Matt seemed serious about the idea.

'I was thinking…' She'd hardly thought about it at all, actually. 'Probably just a couple of pairs of trousers and a few tops?'

Matt grinned. 'Think about it this way. They've told us nothing so I reckon we should be prepared for anything.'

He had a point. 'I'll bring a dress and high heels, then. And whatever else I might need for any situation.'

He grinned suddenly. 'If you don't get to wear the dress, I'll take you to dinner. And don't forget your swimsuit either, the hotel has a really nice pool in the basement.'

Dressing up for dinner with Matt. Hannah was going to have to put in a little more thinking time over her packing.

'You know this place, then?'

'I was there a long time ago. It's a little off the beaten track, but very exclusive. A well-kept secret.'

'One that you know about.' She grinned at him and Matt shrugged.

'Someone's got to. Or they'd never have any guests.'

'All right. Play the man of mystery if you must. I hope your car boot is bigger than it looks, because my luggage expectations have just tripled.'

Matt grinned, taking a sip of his coffee. 'We'll manage.'

They strolled together back to the ambulance parking bays, and Matt took his leave of her. He'd pick her up at two o'clock on Thursday afternoon, along with all the luggage she could manage to wheel down her driveway.

'You two are looking very cosy.' Sophie was waiting for her in the front seat of the ambulance.

'We're teammates.' Hannah felt herself redden. Sophie couldn't possibly understand this. How it was okay to touch Matt's arm and smile when they parted.

'And I thought that *I* was your teammate.' Sophie turned the corners of her mouth down.

'You're my *real* teammate. Matt's just temporary...' Hannah shook her head as Sophie laughed.

'That's okay. I know when I'm beaten. I don't have his outstanding set of attractions.'

'No, you don't.' Hannah decided to play Sophie at her own game.

'Ah, so you admit it. You *are* attracted to him.'

'Who wouldn't be, Sophie?'

Sophie stared at her. 'Then it's one of two things. You're

either sleeping with him already, and not telling anyone, or there's a massive deal breaker in there somewhere. He's not gay, is he?'

'He's not gay, and I'm not sleeping with him.'

Sophie leant back in her seat puffing out a breath. 'So you're not going to tell me, then.'

Hannah laughed. 'There's nothing to tell. We're attracted to each other and I kissed him. But neither of us wants to take things any further, we're just… Neither of us are in the right place for that.'

'You *kissed* him? How was it?'

'It was…fine. Nice.' Beyond describing. 'I'm not going to give you a blow by blow account of it. We like each other, but that's it.'

'That's very adult of you.' Sophie's tone told Hannah that she didn't believe it for a moment. When Hannah thought about it, she'd probably have exactly the same reaction. But that was the way things were with Matt, and she had to make it work.

'I've got Sam to think about…'

'Yeah, yeah. I know. There's nothing like having kids to bring out the adult in you…' The radio on the dashboard burst into life suddenly, signifying the end of their break, and Sophie grabbed it, taking a note of an address and then manoeuvring the ambulance out of its parking space.

'You can't do it, Hannah. You can't fancy the pants off him, and then kiss him, and then just decide that's enough and you're going to stop there. I know you like things neat and tidy, and I'm the last person to blame you for it after what happened with John. But relationships are untidy things.'

It was a piece of wisdom that Hannah didn't need right now. 'Well, maybe this is the way this particular relationship has worked its way through. It's for the best anyway. We need to work together.'

'Right. You just go ahead and believe that.' Sophie

flashed her a grin as she turned out of the entrance to the hospital. 'If it turns untidy, then you know who to call. I promise not to tell you that I told you so.'

Sophie wouldn't need to say *I told you so* because none of this was anything that Hannah hadn't been saying to herself. But when Matt picked her up at two o'clock on Thursday afternoon, his relaxed and cheerful mood was infectious. Sam flung himself at him, and Matt took the time to play with him for a while. Her mother made tea and then Matt took her bags to the car while she hugged Sam, telling him that she'd call him.

'That's okay, Mum. I can go to bed on my own.' Sam sounded as if he had this all worked out. He was testing out his own independence, still needing her but wanting to do things on his own as well.

'Well, I can't. I want to speak to you before I go to sleep.'

'All right, then. I'll be here.' Sam wriggled out of her arms, and ran over to where Matt was putting her bags into the car. 'Bye, Matt.'

Matt straightened up. 'Bye, Sam. Got your victory dance ready for your mum when she gets back?'

The vision of a completely different victory dance floated into Hannah's mind, and she told herself for the hundredth time that it was okay. She and Matt had an understanding.

'Yes.' Sam thought for a moment, obviously bothered by something. 'What happens if you don't win?'

Matt squatted down on his heels. 'We don't need to win, Sam. We just need to do our best. You think your mum will do her best?'

'Yes.' Sam pointed towards the bags in the boot. 'She's taking *all* her clothes with her.'

'Then I'd say she deserves a victory dance when she gets back.' Matt waited while Sam considered the matter.

There would be no rushing him now, he always made time to listen to Sam.

'Yes.' Sam leaned towards Matt, covering his mouth with his hand as he whispered something in his ear. Matt laughed and gave him a nod.

'I think so too.'

There was a bit of rearranging, and squashing of corners, and finally the boot closed with all their luggage inside. Sam and her mother stood in the driveway waving, and when Matt flashed all of the car's lights in response, Sam hallooed. Hannah craned around in her seat, watching until she couldn't see her son any more.

'First time you've been away from him for so long?'

'Yes. I know he'll be fine, but I can't help missing him already.' Hannah settled back into her seat, staring at the road ahead. 'What did he say to you?'

Matt chuckled. 'He told me that he thinks the victory dance makes you happy.'

Hannah couldn't help smiling, and wanting to hug her little boy. 'He sees more than I think he does sometimes.'

'Kids do.' Matt quirked the corners of his mouth down. 'But you're a great mother, Hannah. He sees good things.'

'I hope so.' The better she knew Matt, the more it felt that at some time he'd been made to feel that the world wasn't a good place at all. That he'd had to build his own confidence and sense of security, rather than inheriting it, and that he was always afraid of it slipping away.

But they were Matt's secrets. He had his reasons for keeping them, and he'd told her what she needed to know. She should respect that.

And there was a road ahead. Beckoning them both into something that was both exciting and terrifyingly unknown.

Matt knew this hotel. When his mother had left his father, she'd fled to London. Afraid of staying with any of her family here, in case his father should discover them, they'd stayed here for two weeks. Then moved on to another hotel and then another, until his mother could find a more permanent place to live. Permanent had turned out to be six months.

But this place was special. His mother had explained carefully that they'd needed to leave, but Matt hadn't needed any explanations. His arm had still been in a sling from what his father had done to him, and he knew full well that they were fleeing from fear and pain, and that this was the start of a new life. While his mother had been engaged in meetings with solicitors and those members of her family that she felt she could trust enough to share the secret of their whereabouts, he'd explored every inch of this new world.

He drove past the unassuming entrance, and took a sharp right into the garage, below the building. They unloaded their bags from the car, and took the lift up to the lobby, where a porter immediately stepped forward to take their luggage, seeming almost offended that they'd dared to bring it this far themselves.

It was quiet here. No shouting, no screaming. It felt just the way it had then, like an oasis of calm in the busy heart of the city.

'Hannah… Matt…' A young woman that he'd seen before amongst the TV crew stepped forward. 'You made it. How was your journey?'

She made it sound as if they'd braved hell and high water to get here. This time it had only been fifty miles of motorway and a few traffic lights.

'Good. Thank you.' Hannah smiled at her. 'We're looking forward to the weekend.'

Matt felt her elbow in his ribs, and realised that he should be a part of this conversation. 'Yes. Looking forward to it.'

They were whisked over to the reception desk to sign

the register, and then ushered upstairs. The top-floor suite comprised two bedrooms, on either side of a comfortable sitting room.

'We've booked the whole place out for the weekend, and we have full use of all of the facilities, so make yourselves at home. This suite is your bolthole…' The woman smiled at her own joke and Matt allowed himself a grim smile. The idea of the hotel as a bolthole was more appropriate than she knew.

'There are no cameras here, we've set up a few rooms downstairs with static mounted cameras, and of course the outside broadcast team may be following you at times. But we'll try to keep that as unobtrusive as possible. Dinner's at six, and then there's a meeting, where we'll outline your challenge for the weekend.' The woman smiled apologetically. 'I'm going to need your phones.'

Matt took his from his pocket, handing it over. 'Any last-minute texts, Hannah?'

'Oh. Yes, of course.' She'd been looking around at her new surroundings, and had momentarily forgotten that she'd promised to text her mother when they arrived. 'I just have one more to send.'

'Yes, of course.'

The woman smiled, waiting as Hannah typed furiously. She obviously had a little more to say than just a quick notification of their arrival and Matt reckoned that there would be hugs and kisses for Sam in there somewhere. Finally she gave up her phone, her momentary grimace showing that this might just be the hardest thing she did this weekend.

Their luggage arrived, and was placed in their rooms. And then they were alone. Standing on opposite edges of the large rug that filled the space between the two comfortable sofas.

'What do we do now?' Hannah looked at her watch. 'We have two whole hours…'

'Unpack?' Matt shrugged. 'Relax.'

She rolled her eyes. 'Do you feel as if you could relax? And it'll only take ten minutes to unpack…'

Gold medal for unpacking, then. Hannah had brought four bags with her, and ten minutes sounded like a record-breaking sprint.

'So…let's unpack first. And then decide on a relaxation strategy.'

Hannah was as good as her word. It was nine and a half minutes from when he closed his bedroom door to hearing her knock.

'Aren't you done yet?' Hannah's voice drifted through from the sitting room.

'Uh…nearly.' Matt decided to work out the intricacies of the shirt press later, and stuffed everything that was left in his case into the wardrobe. That would have to do for the time being.

Hannah was bright-eyed and restless. Staying in their suite would be like trying to contain an inquisitive tiger, and he suggested they take a walk around the hotel. They explored the ground floor, finding that the lobby was full now of new arrivals, and slipping away to peer into the dining room and bar, and check out the conference room at the back of the building.

'The pool's that way. And a steam room!' Hannah had caught sight of a sign that pointed towards the staircase that led down to the basement. 'I brought my swimming suit.'

Matt had too, reckoning that a few early morning laps might prepare him for the days ahead. He followed Hannah downstairs.

'Oh, and a gym.' Hannah peered through the glass doors and turned away. 'What a shame. It looks great, but I doubt we'll have enough energy to spare for it.'

A young man in sweatpants and a polo shirt, emblazoned with the name of the hotel, approached them. Hannah smiled, asking him to show them the pool, and he led the way.

'This is gorgeous!' The long narrow pool shimmered under green and blue lights, with Roman-style columns supporting wide beams that ran across the ceiling. The theme continued along the far wall, which was decorated with a mosaic that ran the full length of the pool, and depicted scenes of nymphs, dressed in classical costumes.

'The Pamper Room is open all day, and you can make an appointment for a full session...' The man broke off as Hannah waved her hand dismissively.

'No pampering. But you have a steam room?'

They were shown the steam room, which was tiled in blue and green to match the pool, and big enough to accommodate eight or ten people. Hannah turned to Matt.

'What do you think?'

He thought...that there were many good reasons why he shouldn't spend time with Hannah clad only in a towel. But they had boundaries now. Ground rules. Before he could change his mind again, Matt nodded.

'Yeah. It would be good to relax.'

By the time he left the small dressing room, anchoring the thick white towel securely around his waist, Matt was having second thoughts about this. But leaving Hannah to sit alone, while he made an escape back to his bedroom, was unthinkable. He opened the door of the steam room, finding that she was already there, swathed in a similar towel to his.

He sat down on the tiled bench, opposite hers, leaving plenty of space between them. Keeping his gaze on the floor seemed like a good option, although he could still see her feet, which were already a little pink, presumably along with the rest of her. Matt swallowed down the lump in his throat.

Steam rose between them, and he felt beads of sweat begin to form on his forehead. He should break the silence, but couldn't for the life of him think of anything to say. Then Hannah started to tap her foot...

'All right, I'm going to look. Only you have to look too.'

That was one way of breaking the ice. Suddenly this didn't seem so hard after all.

'Okay. Do you want to go first?'

'No. I think we should do it together.'

Sweat trickled down his spine. He looked up at her, and found that she was unashamedly looking him up and down. Relief washed over him as he realised that Hannah liked what she saw.

He liked what he saw, too. The curve of her shoulders, and her pale skin, flushed with the heat. Her hair was pulled up in a messy bun, but a few strands had escaped and were sticking to her brow. The place where her towel was tucked over itself, between her breasts, was endlessly fascinating.

And this was okay. They'd given each other permission, and he felt no embarrassment. Even the dark scar on the back of his shoulder didn't bother him. Matt was always conscious of it, although few people ever asked about it and those who did accepted his excuses without question. Hannah couldn't see it from where she was sitting, and it suddenly seemed too unimportant to waste any more time on.

'That's got that over with.' He grinned at her and she grinned back. Hannah's chuckle was infectious, and laughing together drove away the last remnants of awkwardness.

'Could I just say—'

'No, you couldn't just say anything.' Matt saw the mischief dancing in her eyes and decided he probably didn't want to hear it.

'All right.' She mouthed the words instead. *Nice shoulders.*

Okay, so he'd been wrong. He did want to hear it.

Fabulous knees, he mouthed back at her, and she laughed.

Hannah leaned back, closing her eyes. Matt took one last

look at her, and did the same, feeling the cool of the tiles against his skin. The image of her smile stayed with him, curling through his thoughts like the subtle scent of pleasure.

CHAPTER ELEVEN

MATT HAD BEEN congratulating himself on not only surviving the steam room but enjoying the chance to relax and laugh a little with Hannah. But when she appeared from her room, dressed for dinner, he found the juxtaposition of two separate images was far more arousing than he'd bargained for.

She wore a slim patterned skirt, with high heels and a wraparound blouse. Hannah looked both elegant and seductive, and when the image jostled in his head with that of one tiny bead of sweat running past the curve of her neck, and down towards her breasts, it was almost unbearably erotic.

This had to stop. It would, as soon as they got started on the challenge. It was just the effect of having too much time on his hands.

They made their way downstairs to the dining room, chatting awkwardly in the lift with two of the other contestants. Dinner was a matter of mostly surveying the room and picking at their food in between times.

'They look...ready for anything.' Hannah nodded towards a table where two men were laughing loudly together.

Matt shook his head. 'Too confident, I reckon.'

'What about them, then?'

He followed her gaze towards two women, who were talking intently, oblivious of everything that was going

on around them. Matt could see the tension in their movements.

'Too nervous.'

She rolled her eyes. 'So what are we, then?'

He leaned towards her. 'We're the dream team. Flash
and Robin.'

That made her laugh. Maybe Flash and Robin could
achieve what Matt felt unequal to at the moment and con-
fine their intimacy to that of friends and teammates.

They were shepherded into a large sitting room, and the
director of the project stood up. The silence was so sudden
and complete that a pin dropping would have made everyone jump. Matt reckoned that you'd even hear the swish
of it on its way down.

'Ladies and gentlemen. Welcome, and I hope you've
all made yourselves comfortable here. We'd like to thank
the Elsynge Hotel for allowing us to set up shop here for
the weekend.' He nodded towards a man wearing a blue
jacket with the logo of the hotel on the breast pocket, who
returned a benign smile, gauged to imply that nothing was
too much trouble.

'You'll be wondering what your task is for the weekend. It's very simple. You all know that the winners will
be taking back a cheque for their hospital. We want you to
produce a presentation of how that money might be spent,
by eight o'clock on Sunday evening.'

There was a hum of whispered conversation, and one
of the nervous women raised her hand. 'What kind of presentation are you looking for?'

The director smiled. 'That's up to you to decide. Show
us what you think we need to see.'

The two confident men were talking animatedly. Hannah turned to him, frowning. 'How are we going to do
that? It's up to the hospital board to say how the money's
spent.'

'I don't know. It's a good question, you should ask.'

She raised her hand hesitantly, and Matt jolted her elbow, pushing it up so that she caught the director's eye.

'I've got a good idea of how I'd like to see the money spent, but it's not my decision. The board of our hospital would be in charge of that.' A hum of agreement went around the room. Matt supposed that all of the other contestants were in much the same position.

'We understand that the final decision belongs to the spending committees of your various hospitals, but this is your chance to influence that. You'll be submitting your presentations on Sunday evening, and on Monday you'll have a chance to talk to the judges. We've invited representatives from each of your hospitals to attend, and see your ideas. This is your chance to speak directly to them, as well as us.'

Hannah flashed a look at Matt. This was real. And it was a responsibility that neither of them had expected.

One of the over-confident guys put up his hand, and stood to ask his question, so that everyone could see him. 'Can we leave the hotel if we want?'

'Yes, you can go anywhere at any time. The only thing we ask of you is that you sign yourselves out, and take along the production assistant who'll be assigned to you. There may also be a camera crew, but they won't accompany you anywhere without specific permission, we don't want to cramp your style. The one thing we need from you is that you don't use your time away from the hotel to contact anyone other than the specific person you're going to see. This is a project that you have to complete alone.'

There were more questions, but Hannah seemed not to hear them, sitting deep in thought. As soon as the meeting broke up, she wound her way through the groups of people still talking in the conference room, and Matt followed her as she hurried back to their suite.

* * *

Hannah felt sick. She'd determined to win the money, and had been happy to leave it to others to decide how it was best spent. But now there were a hundred different areas of need, all jostling for position in her head. It was an impossible decision.

'This is above my pay grade, Matt.' She flopped down onto the sofa.

'Yeah. Mine too.' He sat down, his brow furrowed.

'Maybe we should make a list of all the various departments. Then we could pinpoint their specific areas of need…' Hannah shook her head. That was a terrible idea. 'That alone would take us all weekend. We don't have the time.'

'And I'm not sure it'll get us any further—every department needs something. How would we choose?'

'Pick names from a hat?' She sighed. 'I just can't think of any one thing that's more important than everything else…'

'We should pick something that we love. Something we'd go that extra mile to achieve, because that'll show through in our presentation.'

'Yes, that's good.' Hannah thought hard. 'I wish my head weren't so full of all the different options. I can't stop thinking for long enough to know…'

'Me too.' Matt stared at the ceiling. 'I suppose we could always get drunk.'

Hannah chuckled. 'Yeah. If I'm drunk enough to unclutter my head, then I'll have a twenty-four-hour hangover. That's not going to help much.'

'Exercise?'

Sex.

Happily she hadn't voiced the first thing that flew to mind. But the general principle was a good one, they couldn't plan their way through this. They had to find something that took them out of the mire of pros and cons.

'Exercise sounds good. I'd say running, but my knee's still a bit shaky.'

'What about swimming?' He grinned suddenly. 'Although you might not be able to keep up…'

They'd effortlessly leap-frogged their way to a conclusion, each relying on the other's ideas. This was a good way forward. Hannah got to her feet, making for her bedroom.

'Don't bank on it Matt, if I have to cheat to get ahead of you then I'll have no hesitation in doing so. I'll see you down there.'

Matt was already in the pool when she entered the large, tranquil space. They were alone here, and the empty corridors had attested to the fact that the other contestants were probably in their rooms, busy hammering out ideas. Maybe they should be too, but they'd always relied on each other rather than follow the crowd.

Hannah slipped off her fluffy hotel robe, and got into the pool. Maybe he was watching her, but she felt no self-consciousness. She wanted him to.

'Ready?' He was treading water, ripples splashing over his shoulders. He really did have great shoulders. His skin seemed almost golden under the overhead lights. Maybe exercise would quench the urgent need to touch him, although Hannah doubted it.

'Yes. Ten laps?'

He shook his head, motioning towards the clock above the door to the changing rooms. 'What about ten minutes? No competing, just push at our own personal best.'

Because he knew he'd win. Hannah decided to see his suggestion as generous, rather than patronising, because that was certainly the way he meant it.

'Okay, ten minutes.'

It was ten minutes of hard work. Hannah swam regularly, and it was obvious that Matt did too. When their time was up, he waited for her, bobbing up and down in the water.

'Any ideas yet?'

'Nope. You?'

'Nothing. Another five minutes?'

She nodded pushing off from the side of the pool.

This time she waited for him, because Matt had not only passed her but managed to squeeze extra laps in as well. 'Anything?'

He grinned at her. 'Another five?'

'You're on.'

They were both slowing now. After five more minutes of concentrated swimming, Hannah was tiring and her knee was beginning to throb a little.

'That's enough, Matt. I can't do another five…'

'Me neither.' He swam to the side of the pool, boosting himself up out of the water. It was an exercise in perfection, and Hannah watched as he grabbed the towelling robe from the seat where he'd left it. Then he sat down, waiting for her to collect her robe and join him.

'What have you got?' He picked up a towel, rubbing it vigorously across his head, and Hannah peeled off her bathing cap.

'I've got… Nothing. I'm still out of breath…'

'You've got something. I know you have.' Matt's smile, and the look in his eyes was as intoxicating as when he'd kissed her. Taking her away from everything she thought she knew…

Suddenly a thought shot into her head. 'Sam was born with a cleft lip and palate. You've noticed the scar?'

'Only because I'm a surgeon. Someone did a very good job.'

'Yes, they did. His was relatively minor, but it's more

common than a lot of people realise, about one in seven hundred babies. He had feeding difficulties, though, and it was a struggle for a while. A lot of kids have much more severe problems, ear infections and speech difficulties.'

Matt nodded. 'What kind of project would have helped him?'

'I don't know… The surgery and care Sam had was marvellous. A lot of kids are hesitant about taking solid food, and they and their parents have problems with the way that people treat children with any disfiguring condition.'

'So we concentrate on support, rather than medical treatment. You think that's the best way to spend the money?'

'Yes, I do. We can make more of a difference there, the money will go further.'

'I agree. So we'll go for that?'

He hadn't suggested anything himself. If it were up to Hannah to spend the money, that would be her choice, but this team was made up of two people.

'No. I'll hear your ideas first.'

He shrugged. 'Sam's important…'

'Yes, he is. Come on, Matt, what's important to you?'

'I guess…' Matt thought for a moment. 'Young people like Mia. We have all the facilities to give them the best medical care, but it's difficult for them to stay positive. They have to really stick at the exercises.'

'It would be really good to help them.'

'It would be really good to help kids like Sam, too.'

They were at an impasse. Neither wanted to let go of the projects that were so close to their hearts, but neither could deny the other's. Hannah stared out over the water, the overhead lights reflecting on its surface. It was restful. A luxury that wasn't always available in the busy wards of the hospital…

'A sensory room?' Matt suddenly voiced the idea that had been forming in her head.

'Yes! We could create an area that can be changed to

meet different needs. Anyone benefits from being relaxed and happy, babies like Sam and youngsters like Mia.'

'Maybe a pool…' Matt was grinning now.

'Earth to Matt. That's far too expensive.'

'So what if we build a capacity for expansion into the plan? Raising extra money is a possibility, isn't it?'

'I guess so.' Hannah was almost breathless from excitement. 'I want to start *now*, Matt. I mean this very minute…'

'Me too.' He jumped to his feet. 'You reckon we have our idea?'

'Yes, I do.' A thought occurred to Hannah. 'What do you think the hospital board will say?'

'We can't worry about that. We're both medical professionals, and we understand what's needed and what can and can't be done. We have to just make the decision the best we can.'

'Yes. You're right.'

They'd done it. Together. His ideas and hers, twined together in something that felt like an embrace. Hannah slipped on her canvas shoes, and together they hurried away from the pool and up the stairs.

The media room was locked and she rattled the door handle impatiently. The unit director appeared from the adjoining room, where cameras and microphones were being set up, in readiness for tomorrow.

'Sorry. It's closed until tomorrow.' He was eyeing their robes and grinning.

'We've been swimming. And we need the internet.' Matt returned his stare.

'Like I said. No internet until tomorrow at ten o'clock, we'd like you to spend this evening deciding on your projects. After that you'll have twenty-four-hour access.'

'But we've already decided.' Hannah tried to reason with him and he shook his head.

'Okay. Thanks anyway.' She heard Matt's voice behind her and felt him tug lightly at her sleeve. He was right, no one was going to be allowed into the media room tonight, and they should go back to their suite.

Hannah followed him into the lift, looking up at him dejectedly. 'So what are we going to do now? It's fourteen hours until the media centre opens and we can't start re-searching.'

Matt chuckled softly. 'How about we just dream a little more, then?'

CHAPTER TWELVE

THE HEAT WAS oppressive tonight, and when Hannah had showered off the chlorine from the pool, she slipped on a pair of shorts and a T-shirt. When she walked into their shared sitting room, Matt was on the house phone, just ending a call.

'You managed to get a line out?'

He laughed. 'No, I was just ordering some drinks.'

He was wearing a faded pair of jeans that had been washed and worn until they were like a second skin. She'd seen him work his body so many times now, and there was always something new to like. His strong arms, slicing through the water in the pool, or straining to support his weight when he tackled the climbing wall. Those long legs that seemed to eat up the miles. She'd seen him talking to people and the way that his quiet manner put them at ease, had watched him and Sam discussing the world, nodding solemnly to each other as they came to a conclusion. But her favourite version of Matt was this one. Relaxed and smiling, his eyes seeming very blue against his tan, and sparkling with ideas. She fetched a pad, and started to make a list.

'What do you think about building?' The drinks had arrived and he was swirling his thoughtfully, allowing the ice to clink against the sides of the glass.

Hannah put down her pen. Aspirations were one thing,

but this was way beyond their budget. 'Building. You're serious?'

'I'm not sure yet. But prefabs are low cost and very configurable. We could make a space that was exactly as we wanted it.'

'Prefabs?' Hannah shot him a pained look. 'The only thing I know about prefabs are that my old school had a few of them tacked on to the main building. They were far too hot in the summer and freezing cold in the winter.'

'They've come a long way since then. I worked at a hospital in Glasgow that had some prefabricated wards and they were great. Clean and modern and very comfortable.'

'But…they're too expensive for us, aren't they?'

'Yeah. But what if we could approach a manufacturer, and ask if they'd like to donate to a high-profile charitable project—' Hannah started to laugh and he gave her a reproachful look. 'Hey…this is being filmed for TV, it doesn't get more high profile than that. And lots of manufacturers use donations to gain publicity. It's tax-efficient…'

'You make it sound almost do-able.'

'*Almost* can be stretched a little, can't it? What do you say to phoning round a few suppliers tomorrow and just testing the water. I could do that while you investigate some of the cascade lights you were talking about.'

'Okay. I'll put it on the list.' Hannah scanned the paper in front of her. 'So we have exercise and therapy equipment, different kinds of lights and a sound system, along with a new building and… What about an outside area, where kids can play in the summertime? We could have a play fountain, Sam loves the one in the park near us.' They were moving in the realms of the impossible, and somehow it all seemed possible.

'Sounds good. Anything else?'

'That's enough for the time being. We'll be lucky to get half those things into our budget.'

'Then we have to prepare the presentation. In three days.' Matt chuckled.

'Oh, yes. I forgot the part about the three days.' Hannah grinned at him. 'Maybe we'll have to forgo sleeping.'

'In which case we should probably get an early night. Although I think it's going to be too hot to sleep tonight.'

Dreams and hot nights. And Matt. The man she couldn't have, because they'd both agreed that romance wasn't on their agenda. But maybe fantasy was.

She'd never made the first move before. But the look in Matt's eyes told her that he wouldn't push her away. Even if he couldn't stay with her tonight, he'd make his regret into something delicious, as he had when he'd slow-danced her to his front door. Hannah stood up, walked over to the sofa and sat down next to him.

For a moment they didn't touch. And then he curled his arm around her shoulders, and she snuggled against him.

'This is nice.' She felt him drop a kiss onto her brow. '*Really* nice.'

If she had any doubts, she should stop now. She could stop, and Matt would understand. That very fact chased the what-ifs away. They couldn't change each other's lives, but that didn't mean that the next few hours had to be spent apart. She reached for him, and he was there. When she kissed him, he was so deliciously there that everything else melted away.

'Hannah…' He broke away from her, his eyes dark with desire. 'Are you sure? This can't change anything between us…'

'But do you want it?'

'Can you doubt that?'

She moved closer to him, feeling the strong beat of his heart under her hand. 'Then I'll be plain, Matt.'

'Please. I like it when you speak your mind.'

She leaned forward, whispering in his ear. Words for him alone that made him almost choke with surprise.

'All that? In just one night?'

'If you can't stand the pace…'

'Just try me, Hannah. Only you'll be coming first…' The world tipped as he got to his feet and gathered her up in his arms, carrying her across the room and into her bedroom. There was no stopping him now and…

'Wait! Matt do you have condoms?'

'No.' He hesitated for a split second, and then put her down onto the bed, kneeling in front of her. 'I don't want to wait, Hannah. But I *can* improvise… Trust me, we'll be safe.'

'I trust you Matt.' She reached for the lamp beside the bed, flipping it off. 'We've done this before. Led each other in the darkness.'

He smiled. 'Yes, we have.'

The bedroom gave a stunning view of the city through floor-to-ceiling windows. Matt closed the heavy drapes, shutting out the lights that stretched across the horizon. He was just a shadow now, caught in the gleam of the lamps from the sitting room, and when he shut the door she could see nothing. But he was there. She could feel his fingers caressing her cheek and his lips on hers. He pulled her T-shirt over her head, and Hannah tugged at his jeans and heard the sharp sound of the zipper.

He laid her down on the cool sheets, and she felt his skin, warm and firm beneath her fingers. And then everything seemed to focus on his touch, and the darkness and exquisite pleasure.

Just Matt. Only his hands, and his mouth, finding each and every place that made her shiver. He was guided by each catch of her breath, each whimpering cry that tore itself from her lips. Precise and careful, his fingers showed no hesitation, no mercy as they travelled across her stomach and down between her legs…

Fireworks in the night. Losing herself in the loud

clamour of desire, and then finding him there, still holding her, his body warm and strong next to hers.

'Nice one, Flash…' His lips touched her ear, as he whispered the words and Hannah shivered, aftershocks still running through her body. Her mind was a blank, just pleasure and satisfaction and the warm presence of the man who had given her these gifts.

She could feel his erection, impressively hard against her leg. And then one thought came rushing into the vacuum, urgent and complete.

When she pushed him over onto his back, he let out a groan of relief. Maybe he'd thought she might just curl up in his arms and go to sleep, but that wasn't what teammates did. As her fingers explored, she felt the urgency of his desire, and she whispered in his ear.

'I'm not leaving you behind, Robin.'

Matt liked sex. It was straightforward and uncomplicated, because he always made it that way. But this was different.

Complex, multifaceted, and more satisfying than he'd ever realised. When Hannah had come, it had been a dizzying triumph, marked by her cries in the darkness and the feel of her skin, suddenly burning against his. When she'd tipped him over, making it very clear that she was about to take him where she'd just been, he'd felt profound thankfulness and sudden, unrelenting need.

They hadn't even gone all the way, but it seemed further than he'd ever been before, venturing into unknown territory. If he'd been able to think, that might have worried him, but thinking was out of the question at the moment. He was helpless in Hannah's hands, his body responding to her and only her. He came hard and fast, and in the sudden agony of desire he could hear her low purr of pleasure.

And then came the new pleasure of seeing her. It seemed like another first time, as uniquely pleasurable as the last, standing under the shower together, letting it cool their bodies. He wanted another first time now, more than he'd wanted it before.

'I'll go downstairs…' He kissed her, feeling her hands caress his back, along with the cascade of water. 'I'm sure I saw a condom machine in the cloakroom downstairs.'

'Mmm. We can go all the way next time.'

The thought that there was more propelled him out of the shower and he scrubbed his hair dry, finding his jeans and T-shirt on the floor by the bed where they'd been discarded. Hannah followed him, wrapped in a white bath towel, and the only thing that could slow his haste was stopping to kiss her.

'Hurry up.' She looked up at him, and he found himself transfixed in the warmth of her golden-brown eyes. 'Go…!'

'Then let me go.'

She knew the ties that bound him. Her eyelids fluttered downwards and he was free. Matt threw an exhortation over his shoulder, telling her not to move one inch, and hit the corridor, making for the lift at a run.

When he got back, she was sitting on the bed, still wrapped in the towel. Waiting. He took the packets of condoms out of his pocket, laying them on the side table, and she nodded, smiling. The light from the lamp by the bedside caressed her face.

'Get undressed.' Hannah didn't move. This time she wanted to watch.

As he pulled his T-shirt over his head, she gave a smiling nod, as if she liked what she saw. He was ready for her now, and Matt hoped it wasn't too soon. But as he stripped his jeans off her smile broadened. Hannah stood, letting the towel fall to the floor, watching his reaction. That pleased her too.

Sliding carefully, slowly inside her was a new pleasure, because he could see her face. Moving until they were both lost in the moment. A thin sheen of perspiration began to form on her brow, and he felt sweat trickle down his back.

This time he felt her orgasm. Saw her face, and the way her hair spread across the pillow. It tipped him over the edge as surely as her voice in the darkness had done. Afterwards, they lay for a long time, curled up on the bed, the heat of the night too fierce for anything other than a sheet to cover them.

Finally Hannah moved. 'I'm thirsty. Would you like something?'

'I'll go.' Matt tore himself away from her, putting on his jeans and walking through to the sitting room, where there was a small refrigerator, stacked with drinks. Picking up two glasses, he put them down on the bedside table, leaning over to touch her cheek with the can from the fridge.

'Ow!' She yelped, sitting up and then caught the can from his hand, pressing it against her cheek again. 'That's really nice.'

Heat and cold. Two more opposites to explore maybe. Next time. Matt usually didn't make any promises to himself about a next time, but it was impossible that there shouldn't be one. They had a long, long way to go before tonight was finished.

He sat down on the bed, pouring the drinks, aware that Hannah was watching him. Being watched usually bothered him, but for the moment he couldn't remember why. She took the glass, pulling the sheet up around her.

'I see your shoulder.' She was sipping her drink, looking at him steadily.

Now he remembered. Being with Hannah was like drawing a line between now and then—before Hannah, and after Hannah. But suddenly the past broke through, snapping ferociously at his heels.

Most people didn't even notice the dark mark on the back of his shoulder, and if they did he lied about the cause. The scar was so old now, hidden from his view when he faced himself in the mirror, that he could afford to ignore it. But Hannah had seen more in the way of injuries than most, and anyway telling her anything but the absolute truth would be a betrayal so outrageous that he couldn't even think about it.

'I'm not asking you to talk about it, Matt. But I want you to know that I see it and that…whatever happened to you, I wish it hadn't.'

Her eyes filled with tears suddenly. She knew. But even now, Matt couldn't let go of the secret he'd kept from everyone.

'What do you think happened?' It wasn't fair to ask her to take all the risks, but Matt couldn't go there unless Hannah led him. Maybe she wouldn't. Maybe she'd want to believe that he'd fallen out of a tree when he was a kid…

She moved, pushing the pillows behind her so that she could sit up a little straighter.

'You carry your shoulder a little differently…lower than the other one. That's probably the result of it having been dislocated. It's not that obvious…'

'And…?' It was poor encouragement to go on, but it was all that Matt could give.

'The mark on your shoulder…'

'When did you see that?' Suddenly it was important, and Matt didn't know why.

'Just now. I didn't see it when we were swimming.' She leaned towards him, planting a kiss on his cheek. 'I was enjoying the rest of the view too much.'

That was what he wanted to hear. That Hannah had only just seen this, and that her reaction had been to ask almost immediately. That she'd cared enough to want to know.

'What do you think the mark is?'

'It's a burn, and it looks as if it happened some time ago, probably when you were a child.' She hesitated and Matt nodded her on. 'I saw a mark once that was exactly that shape, when someone accidentally burned themselves with the tip of an iron. I may be wrong…'

'You're not wrong. And it wasn't accidental.'

Her eyes filled with tears. 'I'm so sorry, Matt. I know you don't want to talk about it.'

Suddenly that was all he wanted to do. Hannah had reached in and found his secret, and she'd had the courage to tell him that she knew. The heart to cry for him. Matt curled up on the bed, laying his head in her lap.

'I want to tell you about it…'

She held him, giving him the strength to haltingly begin the story. His father's rage and his mother's tears. The more he talked, safe in Hannah's arms, the easier it became.

'My mother took it all. Until I was eight years old.'

'What happened then?'

'He came home early from work one day. I was in the kitchen with my mother, she was doing the ironing. When she heard the front door slam, she told me to go and play in the garden, and went out into the sitting room. But I didn't. I listened at the door, and heard him shouting at her, about something that had happened at work. I knew what it sounded like when he hit her, I'd heard that often enough before…'

He couldn't go on. Hannah waited, holding him. It would be quite okay if he stopped here, she'd understand. The knowledge gave him the strength to continue.

'For the first time, I didn't try to hide. I ran into the sitting room and attacked him, but of course he was far too strong for me. He picked me up, and took me into the kitchen, locking the door behind us. I could hear my mother, begging him to let me go and promising she'd do anything he wanted if he didn't hurt me. He told me he'd give me something to help me remember that I was never to do that again…'

'He burned you. With the iron.'

'He branded me. It hurt so badly that I struggled and screamed and he yanked me up by my arm and threw me across the room, that's when my shoulder dislocated. Then I heard the sound of glass breaking. My mother had smashed the kitchen door, and she was standing over me, with a spade from the garden in her hands. She told him she'd kill him if he ever laid a finger on me again. She was so different, like...'

He felt Hannah's arms tighten around him. 'Like a mother protecting her child.'

'Yes.' He could imagine Hannah like that if anything or anyone ever threatened Sam. Flaming with rage, like a lioness defending her cub. The thought that what had happened to him would never happen to Sam comforted him.

'That was the last time I saw my father. He walked out of the house, and my mother picked me up and took me straight to the hospital. She was bleeding from the broken glass, and she told them some story and they patched us both up. Then she took me back out to the car, and told me that we were never going back. She left me with a neighbour while she went back to pack a few things, and then we left.'

'It must have been...' Another tear escaped from Hannah's eye. 'I can't imagine how you must have felt.'

'I felt as if we'd escaped. We drove for hours, all the way to London. We came to this hotel, she had family here but she was too afraid to go to them in case my father found us. We stayed here for two weeks, and I thought that this would be the beginning of a new life for us. I'd have friends, and a nice school. Everything was going to be all right.'

It had been just like now. Everything would be all right, if he just stayed here in Hannah's arms. Matt knew he couldn't, that they had serious work to do tomorrow, but he could still believe it for a while.

'It wasn't, of course. My mother's family helped her out, and we weren't short of money. We moved from hotel to hotel, until we got a little house, and then after a few months we heard that my father had found us. We ran, and then he found us again, in the cottage in Wales. After that, we just kept running, never really knowing if he was following or not, but never staying in one place for more than six months.'

'Where is she now?'

'When I went to medical school, she decided to go to France for a year. She loved Paris, and settled there for a while. She wrote a book, loosely based on her own experiences, and to her surprise it sold. That gave her a lot of confidence, and she came back to England and started to get involved with a charity that helps battered women. She got a job as a columnist for a newspaper and... I don't know if she'll ever really mend. But she has a good life now, and she's happy.'

'That's wonderful. I wish you'd tell me what the book's called, I'd love to read it.' Hannah paused, as if she wanted to ask a question but wasn't sure how.

'What?' Matt moved, taking her in his arms. Now that he'd told her everything, she was the one who needed his comfort.

'Will *you* ever mend? You seem to still be moving around.'

'I'm not all that sure how else to live. I've mended my own life with my work.'

'But you won't stay, will you?'

He knew what she was asking. Matt's departure might be soon, if the job in London came through. But that wasn't certain yet, and this wasn't the time for uncertainties.

'No. I won't stay.'

She smiled, reaching up to caress his cheek. 'That's okay. You know that permanence isn't my thing either. Just as long as we'll be friends.'

The thought that wherever he was, he could always just pick up the phone and talk to Hannah warmed him. One thread, to anchor him to the past.

'Always, Hannah. I may walk away, but I'll never forget you.'

A sudden crash above their heads startled them. Then

Hannah grinned. 'Thank goodness. Do you think the storm's coming our way?'

'Let's hope so.' The oppressive heat that had been building up for days now seemed to have loosened its grip a little. Matt got up, drawing the drapes back and opening the sliding doors that were cut into the expanse of glass. There was no balcony outside, just a safety rail, but it allowed cool air to filter into the room. It felt as if the temperature had just dropped by ten degrees.

'Oh! That's lovely.' She ran to his side, throwing up her arms so that the breeze could bathe her body. Then suddenly a sheet of rain started to fall, blowing in through open doors. Hannah squealed, and Matt caught her in his arms, kissing her.

'Matt! Again?' She'd felt his erection harden against her.

It came as a surprise to him as well. Just the thought of his father was usually enough to slake any thought of being close to anyone. But his thirst for Hannah was stronger than that. He felt her move against him, turning desire into blind longing. She wanted more too.

'It's not me. It's you… I can't get enough of you, Hannah.' A thought crossed his mind. 'Ever made love in a storm before?'

'If I have I don't remember it.' She wound her arms around his neck, lifting herself to coil her legs around his hips, in an invitation to *make* her remember it this time.

Thunder still rolled over their heads, feeling as if it was shaking the whole building. Then lightning, bathing the whole room in sudden brilliance. Hannah's kiss was like the touch of a hurricane, dragging him irresistibly into its force.

'Now… Before it goes, Matt.'

He wanted that too. He wanted to hear her scream, carried away with the force of the storm. Everything else was blotted out, and *now* was the only thing that seemed real…

* * *

Hannah woke, shivering in the chill of the breeze from the open doors. The storm had left clear skies in its wake, and sunshine was filtering in through the windows. She pulled the duvet up around her shoulders, snuggling against Matt.

Last night had been life-changing. The force of the storm had been nothing in comparison to the journey they'd made together, and now he was sleeping soundly, his arm slung possessively around her waist. He really had possessed her last night, in every way possible. Head and heart, along with her body.

But there was no time for that today. No time to think about how this couldn't last. They had things to do. She leaned towards him, riffling her fingers through his hair and kissing his cheek as his eyes fluttered open.

'Hey, sleepyhead.' Hannah had hoped for that smile, and it was everything that she wanted it to be.

'Hey, yourself.' He closed his eyes, drawing her close, and then opened them again suddenly. 'What's the time? Did we miss the alarm?'

Hannah twisted around so that she could see the clock. 'Six o'clock. We didn't miss the alarm.'

'That's good.' He closed his eyes again. 'We can take our time. Get up and have breakfast. Maybe review our list, before the media centre opens at ten.'

'Yes. We could.' Hannah snuggled against him, holding him tight, and she saw his lips curve into a smile.

'Or... I think you haven't quite made me your very own creature yet. You might want to seal the deal, so that I do everything you tell today.'

'You're not my creature, Matt.' He could be easygoing when he wanted to be, and that was most of the time. But last night he'd shown a controlled mastery, which had driven her beyond anything she'd thought she knew about sex, and had taken her breath away.

'What am I then?'

Right now he was sleepy and smiling. Hannah knew that could change in an instant.

'You're my…teammate with benefits.'

He chuckled. 'High five…?'

Matt held up his hand, and she grabbed it, kissing his fingers. Finally…finally he opened his eyes again.

'You're thinking we should do this for the team?' He grinned lazily at her.

'No. Just because we want to.'

'My sentiments exactly.' He pulled the duvet back, throwing it onto the other side of the bed in one strong motion. The heat of their bodies would soon counteract the morning chill in the air.

CHAPTER THIRTEEN

Everything went better and faster today. A good appetite for breakfast made it taste delicious and they stayed at the table, ordering more coffee, while they divided up the things they needed to do today. As soon as they were allowed into the media room, they sat together in their cubicle, concentrating on the screens of the laptops in front of them.

'I think the lights are sorted. I've found a place that does them really cheaply, and they're sending me through a quote that's good for sixty days.' Hannah wrinkled her nose. 'Do you reckon sixty days will be enough?'

Matt shrugged. 'We have to win this thing first. Then we can worry about the sixty days.'

'True. How are you doing with the prefabs?'

His lip curled into a teasing smile. 'Not too badly.'

'What? Tell me, Matt!'

He chuckled. 'I spoke to a few companies, and they offered to send me their best quotes. One offered ten percent off the list price, which was still far too expensive for us. So I decided that I needed to go to the top. I called the managing director's secretary at Laurence Construction.'

'And she spoke to you?'

'I said I was a surgeon with an interesting proposition. I thought that a bit of mystery might help.'

Hannah laughed. 'Yeah, okay. Go on.'

'I told her what we were doing, and what we wanted. She said that she'd make some enquiries and get back to me, and I reckoned it was just a polite brush-off. But she called back after twenty minutes, and Sir James Laurence wants to see us. He's not in the office today, but he'd like us to drive down to his home in Sussex tomorrow morning.'

'Really? That's amazing. But do we have the time?'

'It's a risk, but I don't see that we can afford not to take it. I told her that we were being filmed but that I'd tell the production company that we wanted to speak privately, and she said that he'd welcome the cameras as long as there were no microphones.'

'That sounds promising. Surely he won't want us to drive all that way just to say no to us in front of the cameras.' Hannah thought for a moment. 'What do you say we get all our computer work and phone calls done today, then plan a round trip tomorrow to pick up the samples we need and go and see Sir James?'

'Yep. And we can start writing up the budget and the proposal tonight.'

'Sounds good. I suppose we'd better get on with it then.'

They worked until six, eating lunch in their cubicle. Hannah disappeared to make her evening phone call to Sam, and when she didn't appear in the dining room, Matt went to find her. She wasn't in their shared sitting room, but when he went to her bedroom door, he could hear what sounded like crying. Matt knocked, and there was no answer.

'Hannah...?'

'I'll be down in a minute.' Her voice had a brittle, cracked edge to it.

'Can I come in?'

'I'm just combing my hair. I'll see you downstairs.'

Right. After last night, wanting privacy to comb her

hair was the worst excuse he'd heard in a long time. Matt walked over to the sofa, sat down and waited.

It took Hannah ten minutes to comb her hair, or whatever else it was she was doing. When she did appear she rushed towards the main door of the suite, obviously bound up in her own thoughts, and she didn't even see him.

'Hannah.'

'Oh!' She gave a yelp of surprise, and whirled around. Matt could see that her eyes and the tip of her nose were a little pink, which would have been enchanting if they weren't sure signs she'd been crying.

'I didn't see you there.'

'I was waiting for you.'

'Okay, well…are you coming?' She opened the door, giving him a puzzled look when he didn't move.

'No. What's the matter?'

'Nothing.'

Matt rolled his eyes. 'Now I *know* it's something. If it really is nothing you'd tell me about it.'

She frowned at him but closed the door, walking over to sit down on the sofa. 'It's not like my knee, Matt. It doesn't affect the competition.'

'So I'm not allowed to care about it? You've been crying, Hannah. What's the matter?'

'It's Sam.' She capitulated suddenly. 'He left his school project out on the patio last night and it got ruined in the storm. Mum explained to his teacher, but he still got nought out of ten, and he'd worked so hard on it. He was really upset.'

'I'm sorry.' Matt reached for her hand, but she didn't move any closer to him.

'It's one of those things. I dare say he'll have forgotten all about it by tomorrow morning, but he sounded so miserable on the phone. I just wish I'd been there.'

Something else was bugging her, something that she wasn't admitting to. The thought of the storm last night brought with it the vision of their embrace, and Matt knew suddenly that Hannah would never admit this to him. He had to voice it, the way she'd voiced what he couldn't.

'And you were here, having sex. The fact that it was really great sex probably makes it a lot worse.'

She laughed, a tear rolling down her cheek. 'Yes, it does actually. Sorry…'

'Don't be. I know you promised to always be there for him.' That promise meant a lot to Hannah, after what had happened with her father.

'I'm learning that I can't. He's growing up and he wants to make his own way in the world. When I pick him up from school now, I have to wait at the far end of the playground, I'm not allowed to go right up to the classroom door. He says that's just for little kids.'

'It sounds hard. I wouldn't be able to do it. But he knows you're there when he needs you Hannah, and that you'd do anything for him. That's what really matters.'

'Unless I have something else I have to do.' She turned the corners of her mouth down.

'That's just not true. I might not know how to raise a child, the way you do, but I have first-hand experience of this. Kids understand exactly who loves them.'

'Thank you.' She heaved a sigh. 'I'm sorry Matt, after what happened to you this must seem so trivial and stupid.'

'It seems loving. And after what happened to me, it's a joy to see it. Sam's got a happy, stable home and he doesn't know anything about the kind of fear that I felt. That's really important.'

Hannah took his hand, squeezing it. 'I think it might be really important that you can say that, Matt. Thanks for talking.'

She seemed about to stand, and Matt pulled her towards him in a hug. First things first. Dinner could wait for another few minutes. 'If you really want to see him we can go now. I'll drive you home.'

She laughed. 'Don't be crazy. We'll be disqualified.'

'It's like we said before, if we can't keep our values, then all of this is meaningless. If you really need Sam, or he needs you, then we'll go, whatever the consequences.'

He felt her lips brush his cheek. 'Thank you for saying that. I know you'd do it as well. But Sam wouldn't like it one bit, he's as keen for us to win as anyone.'

'Then we won't disappoint him?'

'I won't disappoint *you* either. Come down to dinner now, and then we can get on with what we have to do this evening.'

They worked late into the night, and Matt wondered whether he'd be going to his bedroom alone tonight. Maybe after her call with Sam, Hannah would feel too guilty. But when they finally decided that they needed sleep, she took his hand, pulling him towards her bedroom with a whispered promise that sleep wasn't the only thing she intended.

They were up early, and Matt had gone to his room to dress, his lips still tingling from her kisses. He rescued his shirt from the press, and put on the suit and tie he'd brought. Hannah emerged from her bedroom wearing a slimline sleeveless dress, buttoned at the front, with high heels. She was carrying a matching jacket, and her hair was caught behind her head in a neat, shining fold.

'I really wish you hadn't worn that…'

Dismay registered on her face. 'Why? Do you think I should wear tights? They're so hot in this weather…'

'You look beautiful, and very businesslike. I just want to muss you up a bit again, and those buttons…' Matt leaned in, his hand hovering over the top button on her dress. 'Far too much of a temptation.'

'Ow!' She was clearly pleased with his assessment. 'Keep your hands off my buttons, Matt. You can do whatever you like with them later.'

They had a quick breakfast, drawing enquiring looks

from some of the other contestants, who were mostly wearing jeans or sweatpants. The production assistant who was going with them to ensure they didn't do anything that broke the rules bundled into the back of Matt's car, her phone in her hand, and an outside broadcast van followed them out of the underground car park.

'Thank goodness for air-conditioning.' Hannah stretched her legs out in front of her, looking at the sun beating down on the pavements. 'Our first stop is Streatham. They supply specialist lights, and they're only open in the morning, so we'll have to pop in there on our way.'

It took fifteen minutes for Hannah to look at the lights she wanted, and they left with an armful of brochures and some photographs. Then they drove out of London, picking up the motorway before turning off into winding country lanes. Sir James Laurence's home was nestled in four acres of sunlit garden just outside a pretty village, and they drew up outside the large country house at just before ten thirty.

Matt took their jackets from the hanger inside the car, pulling his on despite the heat. The house was spectacular, a grand entrance at the front and topped by a couple of round turrets and a flag.

'Here goes nothing…' Hannah murmured the words, putting on her jacket and walking uncertainly across the gravelled driveway in her high heels. Matt caught her arm to steady her in pretty much the same way that he would have done if they were scaling a climbing wall, but when she tucked her hand into the crook of his elbow, it felt like something very different. The kind of thing a woman might do after the kind of night last night had been.

A woman in a designer suit, not a hair out of place, was waiting in the large, cool hallway. Hannah stepped inside, smiling. It occurred to Matt that she was so used to walking into different homes and different situations that even this didn't faze her.

'I'm Helena, Sir James's secretary.' Matt recognised

the well-modulated tones from when they'd spoken on the phone yesterday. 'You have a film crew with you?'

'They couldn't keep up.' Hannah grinned at her. 'I dare say they'll be here in a minute. This is the production assistant, Cecile.'

'I'll show you where you can set the cameras up, Cecile. Sir James will be on the terrace, so there's no need for extra lighting.' Helena was clearly used to dealing with everything and anything.

An older woman, dressed in sneakers, jeans and a flowery shirt, hurried towards them. Her blonde hair was perfectly styled, and she carried a pair of gardening gloves, which she laid on the hall table.

'Hannah and Matt!' The woman exclaimed, grabbing Hannah's hand. 'I'm so pleased you could come.'

If Hannah was taken aback by the greeting she didn't show it. She beamed at the woman, giving her hand a friendly squeeze.

'I'm Patti Laurence. I just *love Hospital Challenge*!'

'You've been watching?'

'Oh, yes. Every episode. That little victory dance you do, is that with your son? He's very cute.'

'Thank you. Sam's six—I'd show you the proud mother photos, but they've confiscated my phone for the duration.'

'Oh, really.' Patti shot Cecile a stern look, which she didn't deserve. 'I hardly think you'd cheat. Not after giving up your chance to win to help that man.'

'I'd be tempted to. I really miss Sam, I'd be calling him ten times a day to find out what he's doing if I could.'

'Yes, I can understand that. I was exactly the same with my two when they were Sam's age.' Patti turned to Helena. 'I'll make the tea, dear, the tray's ready in the kitchen. Why don't you deal with the cameras?'

'Yes, of course.' Helena smiled, shepherding Cecile away.

'And, Matt…' Patti smiled at him, shaking his hand vigorously, and then turned back to Hannah, taking her arm. 'This way, dear.'

Hannah had clearly made an impression. That was okay, Matt was happy to take a back seat and watch her. His love of watching Hannah wasn't confined to watching her dress or undress, pretty much everything she did fascinated him.

Patti led them out onto a large terrace, chattering to Hannah all the way about *Hospital Challenge*. She showed them to a set of comfortable wicker seats arranged around a glass-topped table and shaded from the sun.

'I'll just get the tea tray. I won't be a minute.' Patti turned towards the garden, yelling at the top of her voice. 'Jamie! Coo-ee! They're here!'

'Let me help you with the tea, Patti.' Hannah took off her jacket, hanging it on the back of one of the chairs, and followed Patti into the house.

Matt sat down, surveying the garden for any sign of Sir James. Just as Patti and Hannah reappeared, Hannah carrying a large tray stacked with what looked like very fine china indeed, he saw a man in a check shirt and corduroy trousers walking towards him across the lawn.

'There he is.' Patti walked down to the edge of the lawn, waiting for her husband, and Hannah deposited the tray on the table.

'Glad I didn't drop this. It would have been my pay cheque for at least three months.' She sat down on the edge of one of the chairs, her nervousness suddenly visible. 'Patti just happened to mention that Sir James likes it when people get to the point. We don't need to try to persuade him, just show him what we have.'

Matt nodded, taking off his jacket and draping it over the back of his seat, feeling the cool breeze with a sense of relief. This heat wasn't conducive to formality. Hannah looked cool and calm as she rose to shake Sir James's hand. White haired, his face lined and tanned, he seemed kindly and welcoming, but his piercing blue eyes were that of a canny businessman.

Patti poured the tea and pushed the plate of biscuits towards them. Helena appeared with a leather portfolio, handing it silently to Sir James, and he smiled and thanked her, glancing towards the camera crew who were standing at the other end of the terrace, waiting for something to happen. Helena turned and signalled to Cecile that they could start filming now. This all seemed effortless but it was organised down to the last detail.

'Are you staying, dear?' Sir James turned to his wife.

'Of course I am. This is *Hospital Challenge...*' Patti shot him an outraged look.

'Yes. Of course.' Sir James turned to them and his smile faded, replaced by an air of businesslike efficiency. 'Tell me what you have so far. And what you need.'

Hannah glanced at Matt and he nodded her on. She was doing just fine so far, and he didn't see any point in messing with perfection.

Hannah started to talk. She pitched straight in, telling him a little about her own experience with Sam, and saying how much she would have appreciated a facility like this. Then she widened it out, speaking about how a sensory room might benefit all kinds of children, and outlining briefly the kinds of activities and therapies that could be carried out there. Her enthusiasm shone through, and somehow she managed to ignore the fact that Sir James was clearly weighing and calculating the worth of each word she said.

'We have a very preliminary plan...' She turned to Matt, and he handed her the folder they'd brought, containing the pages they'd printed out at midnight last night.

Sir James studied the sheets carefully. Patti smiled and offered them both a biscuit.

'It's taken you under two days to do this much?' Sir James put the folder back onto the table.

'I'm a mother, and I've been an ambulance paramedic for six years. Matt's been working as a surgeon for ten. That's how long this has taken us.'

Great answer. Sir James obviously liked it a lot too, as he allowed himself a brief smile before he turned, looking around him. Helena appeared suddenly at his side.

'The microphones are off, they're just filming a few long shots of the meeting.' She anticipated his question and Sir James nodded.

'Thank you, Helena. Will you arrange for them to have some tea, please?'

'Of course, Sir James.' Helena hurried away and Sir James picked up the leather portfolio from the table, unzipping it.

'This is what I can offer you. It's our newest design, and I'm very proud of it. It's built with a close to zero carbon footprint, and it's a configurable space that includes underfloor heating and air-conditioning for days like these.' He handed a glossy brochure to Matt. 'Page six for the plan and an artist's impression.'

Matt flipped thankfully past the building specifications, which meant very little to him. When he got to page six, he saw Hannah's eyes widen. The L-shaped, timber-framed building looked stunning, and there were diagrams showing how the space could be converted to suit practically any requirement.

'We're exhibiting this at a show in a couple of weeks' time. After that it'll be taken down and we'll have no use for it. It would be a shame to consign it to a skip.'

'This is…beyond anything we'd imagined.' Matt spoke first, because Hannah was still staring, lost for words.

'Too big? If you can't fill the space, then…' Sir James shrugged, the steel in his eyes glinting. Matt saw Hannah sit a little straighter in response to the challenge.

'We can fill it. And there's plenty of room for a facility

like this, the hospital has a large open space at the back. I suppose we'd need planning permission, but…'

'I can help you with that.' Sir James smiled suddenly. 'Our planning department nurtures an excellent relationship with local authorities around the country, and our building specifications are tailored to exceed the requirements of planning regulations. With any luck, it shouldn't be a problem.'

Matt doubted that Sir James left anything to good luck. Hannah glanced at him and he nodded.

'Sir James, this is incredibly generous of you. All we can do is thank you, and say yes. We'd very much like to take you up on your offer.' Hannah hesitated, staring down at the brochure, and then her back straightened. Matt sensed that something amazing was coming and waited to hear what it was.

'If we don't win, then we won't get the money to fit this building out. But I can raise the money for a less ambitious scheme, and I'll approach the hospital board and persuade them to accept it. Would it be too presumptuous of me to ask if you'd consider donating this building anyway? Even if we don't win?'

Matt could have hugged her. Hannah had come a long way in the last six weeks, and had gained the confidence to make her ambitions work. Sir James laughed suddenly, flashing a glance at his wife.

'I like your plan very much. What do you think, Matt?'

'I…' Matt spread his hands in a shrug. 'I've learned one thing over the last six weeks. If Hannah says she'll do something, she'll find a way to do it.'

'That's agreed, then. Although I'm sure we're both looking forward to seeing you win, eh, Patti?'

Patti rolled her eyes, smiling at her husband. 'Of course we are. I'm so thrilled we can be a part of it.'

Sir James threw off the persona of a hardheaded businessman, becoming an avuncular host. Patti called towards the kitchen, asking for more tea, and Hannah drank hers thankfully, sitting quietly as Matt answered Sir James's questions about how the building should be configured to best suit their purposes. Patti joined in with the conversation, obviously keen for them to stay as long as possible, and Matt listened carefully to her suggestions.

'You've both been very generous with your time and hospitality. We should be on our way.' Finally he drew the conversation to a close, and Patti grimaced in disappointment.

'Of course you must.' Sir James squeezed his wife's hand. 'We can go and see the project when it gets underway, darling.'

'Yes, we'd love you to come and see us. I'll bring Sam along and we'll show you around.' Patti brightened visibly at Hannah's words.

'I'd love that. Wouldn't you love it, Jamie?'

Sir James chuckled. 'Yes, I would.'

There was an unobtrusive movement, from the other side of the terrace, as the camera crew started to pack up their equipment in response to Helena's chivvying. Sir James walked through to the front door with them, and shook Matt's hand.

'Thank you so much. This is an incredible gift, and it'll help a lot of people.' Hannah held her hand out, and their host grasped it between his.

'I should thank you, Hannah. Patti had a heart attack three years ago, in the middle of the night. An ambulance came, and the two young men were...' He shook his head, as if words failed him.

Hannah nodded. 'They made a difference.'

'They were wonderful. So kind and good humoured. They whisked me off to the hospital, and I had a couple of stents put in.' Patti confided the information to Matt, plainly considering stents as part of his territory.

'And you're fully recovered?'

'Oh, yes! I've got more energy than I had before!' Patti beamed at him.

Sir James was hanging on to Hannah's hand, and she leaned forward a little, putting her free hand onto his. Matt knew that look, and the silent invitation to say exactly how he felt. If Sir James could resist it he had more steel in his heart than Matt did.

'I shook their hands. I didn't have the words to thank them properly, I was so worried about Patti. I've always regretted that omission.' Sir James's words were directed at Hannah.

'Trust me, they knew. Seeing a loved one suffer a heart attack is frightening and distressing, and when someone manages to overcome that to shake my hand, it means everything to me. That, and Patti's recovery is all the thanks that they could want.'

Sir James nodded, letting go of Hannah's hand. He was a man of few words, but he felt this deeply. He put his arm around his wife, and the couple bade them a cheery goodbye.

'I'm going to hug you. Just as soon as we have a moment alone.' Matt murmured the words as he offered Hannah his arm across the gravel.

'I'm going to hug you back.' She turned to give a final wave to their hosts as Matt opened the car door for her. 'What nice people.'

'You gave Sir James a reason to be generous. I'm proud of you.' He settled himself into the driver's seat, waiting for Cecile to come running across from the outside broadcast van and get into the back seat of the car. 'Where now?'

'Fulham. There's a shop there that does all the different kinds of specialist seating that we might need and I'd like to try some of them out. Then back to the hotel. I think we can specify the rest of the specialist equipment from the internet.'

Matt pulled out of the driveway. The stakes were higher now. Hannah had worked so hard for this, and she'd stepped out of her comfort zone when she'd come here. They had to win.

CHAPTER FOURTEEN

BY THE TIME Sunday evening rolled around, Matt and Hannah had been working flat out since the media centre had opened on Friday morning and they were both exhausted. Hannah had made the presentation boards, and Matt had worked through the spreadsheet, making sure they were within their budget. They'd printed off the requisite fifteen copies of their detailed presentation and bound them, and they were ready by seven o'clock. She'd called Sam and then joined Matt up in their suite.

'How's he doing?' He was sprawled on the sofa, and Hannah moved his leg so that she could sit down, leaning against his knee.

'He's good. Mum took him to the zoo today, and he had a great time.'

'That's nice.' Matt's eyes were almost closed, and Hannah's were sore and prickling from lack of sleep as well. 'Is it too early to go to bed?'

'No. Considering we had two hours' sleep last night, I think it's acceptable. I think I feel worse than if I'd worked straight through.' Hannah yawned.

'Nah. A few hours is better than nothing. Will you take it the wrong way if I take you into the bedroom, rip all of your clothes off and then go to sleep?'

'You've got the energy to rip my clothes off?' Hannah teased him.

'No, not really. On second thoughts you might have to do that yourself. Finishing the presentation is about as much gratification as I can take tonight.' Matt gave her a lazy smile. 'I may well feel differently in the morning.'

Sleep and then Matt's embrace. It sounded like heaven. 'Thank you, Robin. For everything. I wouldn't be here without you.'

'Thank *you*, Flash. I wouldn't be here without you.'

Monday had been set aside for the judges to talk to the competitors about their projects, and there was also time to see the other teams' proposals. Their phones had been returned, and Hannah couldn't wait for Sam to get home from school so that they could video call and she'd be able to show him what she'd been doing, and where she was staying.

The hospitals that were competing had sent representatives to discuss the proposed projects with the judges, so that they could assess their viability. Hannah saw Matt with Dr Gregson, the chairman of the hospital board, the two men chatting affably as they made their way across the room towards her.

'Hannah.' Dr Gregson held his hand out to her. 'You and Matt have made the most wonderful effort for the hospital. We're all enormously grateful to you both. Win or lose.'

'Thank you.' Hannah took his hand, feeling her ears burn.

'Hannah's come to an arrangement with Sir James Laurence.' Matt was grinning.

'You have?'

She would have preferred a little more time to decide how to put this to Dr Gregson, but he was here now, and obviously pleased with what they'd done. Matt was right, she should strike while the iron was hot.

'I asked him whether he'd be willing to donate the prefab if we didn't win the contest. We wouldn't be able to afford to do everything we'd planned, but I told him that I'd raise the money for the sensory rooms myself. If you and the board will agree to it, that is.'

'That's very enterprising of you.' Dr Gregson thought for a moment. 'You have my full support, Hannah. I'm sure the other members of the board won't need a great deal of persuasion either, I've already spoken with some of them on the phone and they're delighted with your ideas for the project.'

'Thank you.' Hannah heaved a sigh of relief.

'Of course it may not be necessary.' Dr Gregson smiled. 'I may be biased, but your project is the best I've seen. We'll speak again when we find out whether you've won.'

Dr Gregson took his leave of them, and Matt turned to her, smirking. 'That wasn't so bad, was it?'

'It was horrible, Matt! I could kick you.'

He assumed a look of innocence. 'Why? You didn't have time to get nervous about what you were going to say. And you were perfect, just as you were when you charmed Sir James into giving you a prefab.'

'He didn't give it to me, he gave it to the hospital. And anyway *I* didn't charm him. Our project speaks for itself.'

'It speaks with your voice.' Matt's confidence in her always made Hannah smile. 'I'm going to go and check my email. Will Sam be home from school yet?'

Hannah looked at her watch. 'Oh, yes. I'd better call him now, before it's time for the results to be announced...'

Matt's email had obviously contained something that had soured his mood. When Hannah took her phone upstairs so that Sam could say hello to him, he was sitting, staring at the wall. He cheered up a little to talk to Sam, but Hannah was sure that his smile wouldn't last for long after she left him to give Sam a guided tour of the swimming pool and the gym in the basement.

When she arrived back in the conference room, he seemed cheerful enough. They sat and waited as the final preparations were made, and he curled his fingers around hers. They were both nervous, but being nervous together somehow made it all right.

Finally the chairman of the judging panel picked up the microphone, and a heavy silence fell. Hannah could feel a bead of sweat running uncomfortably down her back.

'I'm going to keep this short, because everyone wants to know who the winners are. But I want to thank everyone here. The projects you've created in a very short time have all shown imagination and flair, and a sound understanding of what your various hospitals need. I gather that a number of your projects will be going ahead, win or lose, and I can only applaud the determination and resourcefulness of all the contestants here this afternoon...'

Get on with it. *Get on with it.* Hannah shot Matt an agonised look and he squeezed her hand.

'And now our winners. Hannah and Matt from Hamblewell Hospital.'

She couldn't breathe. She was going to have to stand up and walk to the podium, but her legs wouldn't carry her. Applause started to ripple through the room, and it swelled into a cacophony of sound in her ears.

'One last push, Flash...' She heard Matt's voice in her ear, and it gave her strength. He rose, following her to the end of the row of chairs and walking beside her to where the judges were waiting to greet them.

She lost count of the number of hands that she shook. The chairman of the judges handed her a large, golden envelope, and she didn't dare look inside to make sure that this was real. Matt took the microphone, thanking everyone, and then turned to her.

'I'm not going to ask Hannah to say anything, because I'm not sure that she can...' He grinned at her as a rumble of laughter spread around the room, and Hannah mouthed a silent, *Thank you.* She'd only make a fool of herself if she took the microphone now.

'I do want to say one thing, though. This last six weeks has been challenging and the person who's challenged me most is my teammate. Thank you, Hannah, for being my partner, my guide and my inspiration.'

She could feel tears rolling down her cheeks. Matt put his arm around her shoulders and she clung onto him. There were more hands to shake, and when Dr Gregson came to congratulate them she pressed the envelope into Matt's hand for safekeeping. Drinks were passed around, and she took a sip of champagne, feeling too dizzy to drink the rest of it.

Finally the gathering began to break up. The contestants who came from further afield were going to be staying on at the hotel tonight, but those whose journeys home were shorter were already leaving. She saw Matt signal to her, and followed him out of the room and up to their suite.

'We did it, Matt!' As soon as the door closed behind them she flung her arms around him. 'I can't believe it, I'm so happy.'

'Yeah. We did it.' He'd been smiling and relaxed downstairs, but suddenly he seemed more tense. Maybe he was thinking about the drive home.

Or maybe he was thinking about *being* home. Back to reality. The last four days had been a fantasy, and neither of them had had time to think ahead. But now they had to, because the bubble was about to burst, and when it did they'd have to face all of the issues that threatened to tear them apart.

But they'd won. That had seemed impossible but they'd done it together. They could do this too, if they wanted to. She could show Matt that his father hadn't irrevocably soured his life.

'Would you like to go home?' He was smiling but his eyes had lost their fire.

'Yes, I would. Thank you.'

He nodded, turning away from her. 'I'll finish packing my things. Will you be ready in half an hour?'

They took their leave of everyone, thanking the production team once again and shaking the hands of the contestants who hadn't left yet. Matt drove in silence, all of his concentration on the road ahead.

Hannah would wait. They could talk when they got back, and she'd tell him. She could be there for him, if only he'd be there for her. As they turned off the motorway into familiar roads, she began to feel more calm, more certain of what she wanted. This couldn't be an ending for her and Matt.

He drew up outside her house, looking at the front door, seemingly deep in thought. Hannah turned to him.

'Should we talk?'

'Don't you want to go and see Sam?'

'He'll be in bed, asleep. I didn't know what time we'd be back, so I told him that I'd be late and that I'd see him tomorrow. He'd only try to stay awake otherwise.'

Matt nodded. 'We should talk. Soon.'

'Why don't I take my bags inside, and we can go for a walk?' The evening was still warm, even though the light would be fading soon.

'Yeah. That sounds good.'

He took her bags from the boot, carrying them to the door. Hannah's mother was waiting for them, and she whispered that Sam had decided that the sooner he went to sleep, the sooner tomorrow would come, and had gone to bed as soon as he was told. Matt waited in the hall while Hannah crept upstairs to see Sam and to blow a kiss to her sleeping boy.

Her mother hugged her, telling her how proud she was of her, and then let her go. Hannah led Matt along the path that meandered past the houses and down towards the stream that ran along the border between the village and the open countryside.

'Matt, I know we said there would be no strings, and that suited us both. But that doesn't mean we have to be strangers…' That was a good start. If they could agree on that, then they could agree to be lovers, too.

She heard him catch his breath and didn't dare look at him.

'Hannah, I'm leaving.'

'What!' This *had* to be a joke. But when she turned to him, his face was deadly serious. 'Leaving…where? Where are you going?'

'I've been offered a job in London.'

Hannah took a breath. That didn't help. 'And you didn't tell me? Matt, you slept with me, and you didn't say anything?'

'I didn't know. The offer was there when I picked up my email this afternoon.'

'What, and someone just offered you a job out of the blue? You must have known it was a possibility.'

'I didn't know whether I'd get it or not. But, yes, it was a possibility. I've been thinking of moving on for a while now.'

'And you said nothing? You said a lot of things, but you didn't tell me that.'

'You knew I couldn't make a commitment, Hannah. You can't either. We both said it. No strings.'

'Yes, we said no strings. We didn't *do* no strings, though, did we…?' Hannah was almost breathless with anger.

'No. We didn't.' He shoved his hands into his pockets, looking at the ground. 'I'm sorry.'

'Well, *sorry* just won't do it, Matt. You know I can't just pick up sticks and follow you…' Hannah felt tears prick at the corners of her eyes. No one had said anything about her following him. She'd betrayed what she really wanted to do, at just the time when she should have kept quiet about it.

'I know. You have Sam and your mother to think about. I'd never ask you to come with me, it's not fair.'

'Then why do you have to go?'

'Because... You know why, Hannah. I didn't believe that I could love you, but I do. And I'm no good at loving anyone...'

'That's no excuse, Matt. If you loved me, then you wouldn't have to worry about whether you were good at it or not, you'd just *be* good at it.'

He looked up at her, and suddenly Hannah saw the unfairness of it all. She was blaming him for something that wasn't his fault. Matt was struggling with a terrible legacy of pain, and he couldn't break free of it. And all she could do was harangue him for it.

'Then maybe I don't love you after all.'

His quiet words cut deep. Shaking with the shock of them, Hannah turned, running away from him. Running away from the man that she'd loved who'd hurt her so very badly.

Maybe he'd follow. She reached her front door, turning to look behind her, and cruel hope tore at her as she saw his shadow, moving towards her. But he was just walking back to his car, and Hannah watched as he opened the door and got inside. After a pause, the lights flipped on and he drove away.

She couldn't go inside, not yet. Hannah wiped the tears from her face, trying to compose herself, but it was no use. She walked around the side of the house, sitting down on the steps that led up to the patio, allowing herself to cry in the darkness.

'You're putting a brave face on something.' Sophie was resting her arms on the steering wheel of the ambulance, tapping her fingers fitfully. Hannah really wished she'd stop it, her nerves were already on edge. 'You can do that with Sam, I guess that probably goes with the job. You can do it with your mum if you want to, but you can't with me.'

Hannah rolled her eyes, unwrapping her sandwiches. 'Why not?'

'Because I have to put up with you all day. And I'm your friend. What happened, Hannah?'

'I'm just a bit tired. It was a tough weekend.'

'Yes, and you've had three nights to sleep it off. And you won, doesn't that make you happy?'

She'd won nothing. The whole hospital seemed to be celebrating, and it seemed like something that had to be endured.

'It doesn't make you happy, does it?' Sophie clearly wasn't going to give up.

'No.' Hannah sighed. Sophie was going to find out sooner or later. 'Matt's leaving. He's got a job in London.'

'What?' Sophie stared at her.

'Yeah. That was my reaction. We had a…thing. And then when we got back, he told me that he was leaving.'

'Just like that?'

'Pretty much.'

'He had sex with you. Then he told you he was leaving.' Sophie's lip curled. 'Just give me ten minutes with him, Hannah. I'm going to hurt that guy.'

'No. You're *not* going to hurt him.' Matt had been hurt enough, and the urge to defend him was stronger than any of the pain that Hannah was feeling. 'He has his reasons. He's never stayed in one place for very long, he just can't do it, and I knew that.'

'What reasons?'

'Good ones.' Hannah turned the corners of her mouth down. She wanted to tell Sophie, but that would be a betrayal. She raised the sandwich to her lips and her stomach began to lurch. She'd been going through the motions of eating and sleeping for the last three days, and doing little of either.

'Does he think that you'll follow him?'

'He knows all about John. If I go with him, then I'd feel that I was putting Sam and my mum second, and he knows I can't do that again.'

Sophie considered the idea for a moment. 'Your mum just wants the best for you, you know that. And if you wanted to move to London, then...lots of people move and their kids don't fall to pieces over it. Sam would probably really like it there, and it's only thirty miles. It's practically a commute, lots of people live around here and work in London.'

'That's not the point, Soph. I'd hate myself, and no relationship can survive that.'

'You've thought about it, though, haven't you?'

'I've thought about nothing else. And I can't do it.'

Sophie puffed out a breath. 'Maybe we should go for a long run. Sweat him out of your system. Or we could go out and get very drunk.'

Hannah laughed. 'Or stay in and get very drunk.'

'That'd work.' Sophie turned to face her. 'You love him, don't you?'

'Yes, I love him. Are you going to say *I told you so*?'

'No, that's a fat lot of use. I'm just here to cheer you on, Hannah. Whatever you decide to do.'

'Thanks, Sophie. That means a lot.' Hannah leaned over, hugging her friend, and Sophie squeezed her so tight that she could hardly breathe.

She had everything, right here. Sam, her mother. Good friends like Sophie. She could work on forgetting Matt and everything would be the way it was before.

It sounded easy. Just as long as she left out the part about Matt having changed her for ever.

Did any of the old rules still apply? Hadn't Matt shown her that life wasn't all about what she couldn't do? It was about what she *could* do.

CHAPTER FIFTEEN

'MAYBE I DON'T love you after all.'

As soon as the words had left his lips, Matt had known that they were a stupid, cruel lie. He'd walked away because he'd been convinced that a clean break would somehow be easier. That if Hannah hated him, then perhaps she wouldn't be hurting as badly as he was.

All the same, he couldn't let it go. He couldn't leave without saying goodbye to her and Sam. And somewhere, deep in his consciousness, it occurred to him that if he and Hannah could win *Hospital Challenge*, they could find a way to make this right and be together.

Maybe he should start with flowers. But none of the bright blooms in the florist's shop were good enough for Hannah. And anyway, a gift carried with it the expectation of forgiveness, and the very most that he could ask of her was that she hear him out.

After a week of trying to think of the right things to say, he decided that there was no right thing. He just had to apologise to her, and find out whether there was any chance that they could move forward from that. Friends, lovers. Exes who didn't hold a grudge. He'd take anything that Hannah felt able to give.

He drew up outside her house just as it was getting dark. It was Hannah's mother's book club evening, and Hannah's car stood alone in the driveway. Sam must be going to bed about now, so he'd get a chance to speak with Hannah alone. It took a couple of minutes to screw up his courage, and his heart was pounding as he got out of the car, walking towards the front door.

Then he saw it. The lights flipped on in the sitting room, and Hannah appeared with Sam, who was in his pyjamas and ready for bed. Sitting down in one of the armchairs, she took him on her lap and opened a storybook.

Matt could almost feel the warmth between them, radiating out into the cool of the evening. He stopped, stock still, watching. It was all he'd ever wanted, and yet...

If by some miracle he did manage to make things right with Hannah, what would happen next? His father had hurt his mother, and then made things right, in a cycle that had turned into years of agony. One of the things his mother had always impressed on Matt was that apologies weren't enough, and that a person had to be truly committed to change.

He wanted to change. But what if he couldn't?

Standing in the darkness, he suddenly saw it all very clearly. Hannah had all she needed, and he should go. He should let her live her life, and find someone who loved her in the way that she deserved.

Thinking of Hannah with someone else brought a bitter taste to his mouth. Matt turned, shaken by the knowledge that however much he wanted to see Hannah again, the best thing he could do for her was to leave. He hurried back to his car, fumbling with the keys and dropping them in the footwell.

A few more moments. Just to be near her. He stared at the light in the window, like a moth drawn to a flame.

He didn't know how long he sat there, but when he saw her tiny figure move, and then the light upstairs flip on, he knew that he had to go before he was tempted by the knowledge that Sam would be in bed and Hannah was alone. Picking up his keys, he started the car and drove away.

* * *

It had been four weeks. Matt had confined himself to the surgical suite while he'd worked out his notice at the hospital, and hadn't seen Hannah. Clearly she didn't want to see him, and there was nothing else to do now but pack the last of his things and leave. Matt was going to be house-sitting for a friend for a couple of months, which would give him time to find a place of his own, and he'd already boxed up one car load of his possessions for storage. The rest would fit in the boot of his car. Matt travelled light.

The thought had always made him feel free. But freedom didn't mean a great deal any more without Hannah.

The doorbell rang and he ignored it. In his head he was already gone, and there would be no one stopping by to bid him farewell. If someone wanted to sell something, they'd have to find another, more receptive customer.

He busied himself, collecting up the last of his possessions from the sitting room, ready to be wrapped and packed into a cardboard box. The sound of a car alarm came from the street. *His* car alarm.

Matt grabbed his keys and looked out of the window. Hannah was leaning against his car, her arms folded, looking up at him. She had that determined look about her that he loved so much.

She gave him a wave and walked towards the front door of the block of flats. Matt swallowed down the temptation to lean out of the window, and shout down to her to ask what on earth she thought she was doing. Hannah had obviously made up her mind that she wanted to see him, and if he didn't let her in he guessed that she'd only go back to his car and set the alarm off again. He almost wanted her to…

The doorbell sounded, and he pressed the Entryphone. He heard the front door slam shut, and counted the beats of his heart until he reckoned she'd reached the top of the stairs. When he opened the door of his flat, he saw her walking towards him.

'What are you doing, Hannah?'

'All of your windows are open and your car's outside.' She smiled at him, and Matt's stomach lurched. 'I guessed you were in.'

'I was busy. And I wasn't expecting anyone.'

'Good. So we won't be interrupted.' She didn't wait for him to ask her in, brushing past him and walking straight through to the sitting room. Matt closed the door and followed, and she swiped a piece of packing material off the sofa so that she could sit down.

'You owe me an apology, Matt.'

She was giving him a chance. Suddenly it wasn't so very hard to apologise, because this was nothing like the way his father had used his apologies to manipulate his mother. Hannah was in control, and asking for something that was rightfully hers.

'I didn't tell you that I had plans to leave. It was wrong of me, and I apologise.'

She nodded. 'Accepted. Although I was at fault too, you told me that leaving was on your agenda and I didn't take you at your word. Is there anything else?'

He knew what she wanted to hear. It was the thing he most wanted to say.

'I told you that I didn't love you. I thought it might make things easier, but...' Matt shook his head, moving a cardboard box from the armchair, and sat down. 'It wasn't true and I'm sorry. I know I hurt you and I don't expect you to forgive me.'

'Thank you. I needed to hear that.' Somehow Hannah didn't seem hurt. She didn't seem beaten. She had that light in her eyes that ignited when she faced a challenge.

'Thank you for the opportunity of saying it.'

Nothing had changed. *Everything* had changed. The fear of seeming like his father had dissolved suddenly and Matt was his own man. His head began to swim.

'I've come to tell you something, Matt. Just so you know.'

He'd listen. Whatever it was that Hannah wanted to get off her chest, he'd take it. Matt nodded her on.

'I've thought about this a lot, and when I heard that yesterday was your last day at the hospital, I had to make a decision.' She took a deep breath, as if there was no going back now. 'I promised myself I'd never follow anyone again, but that was before I fell in love with you. So wherever you go, I'll follow. Whenever you want me, I'll be there.'

Bright, blinding light. Suddenly everything was in sharp focus and the world seemed full of colour. Maybe he'd died and gone to heaven. Matt pulled himself together.

'Hannah, you can't.'

'Try me.'

He shook his head, trying to clear it. 'What about Sam? And your mother…?'

'Mum and Sam are staying here, and so am I. But my heart will always go with you. It'll wait, and if you ever want me…' Her face crumpled suddenly and she clasped her hands together. 'If you *do* want me, then you should call.'

He wanted to hold her. Matt wanted to forget all of the reasons that they couldn't be together and plunge into the fantasy of being with Hannah. But this was real. She was serious about this, and there were real obstacles.

'I want you every day. I love you…' Matt shook his head. 'But this isn't the smart thing to do, Hannah, you and Sam deserve more than I know how to give.'

'We both know how to change. It's just a matter of whether we want to enough.'

Matt's world crashed down around him. Everything that he'd thought he knew, everything that had made it so impossible for them to be together. Hannah had done the impossible, and smashed through it all. He got to his feet, kneeling in front of her.

'Hannah, you're the bravest, most beautiful woman…' She started to cry suddenly, and he reached to brush away her tears.

'You said that I should call you when I was ready. I'm calling you now. I don't know how I can ever begin to deserve you, but I'm going to find a way. I want to be the one that loves and protects you, and Sam, for the rest of my life.'

She threw her arms around his neck. 'Neither of us has to do it alone, Matt. If we stick together we can do all the things we thought we'd never do.'

'Flash and Robin. Ready to take on anything.' He kissed her, holding her as if he was never going to let her go. There was no *as if* about it. He never was going to let Hannah go.

EPILOGUE

Six months later

IT HADN'T BEEN EASY. But that had never stopped them before.

Love had carried them through it all. The therapy, where Matt had begun to shake off the burden of his childhood trauma. His long commute between Hamblewell and London, and the lonely nights when Matt had stayed over at the hospital.

Hannah's fears for Sam and her mother had turned out to be unfounded. Sam loved Matt, and had begun to wonder aloud whether marrying his mum might make Matt his father. Hannah's mother had dismissed the suggestion that she might like to live with them, saying that she had a life of her own now. Wherever Matt and Hannah decided to make their home, she'd visit regularly. Sophie had promised to do so as well, when she wasn't busy with her A and E doctor. Hannah had confided to Matt that she thought that Sophie's days of serial dating were over.

Wanting to know more about Matt's childhood, Hannah had read Matt's mother's book from cover to cover and been moved to tears by it. The two women had liked each other immediately when Matt had taken Hannah and Sam down to Devon to visit, and the warmth of his mother's welcome had left them in no doubt that she was delighted to see her son finally settling down.

The weekend in Tuscany, when Matt had proposed to her, had been wonderful. They'd stayed on a secluded beach, eating, swimming and making love for two days, and when they'd arrived back home, Matt had asked Sam if he could be his dad.

And it had all led them here. To the doorstep of a house in a leafy suburb of London, which backed onto a park. There was a great school, just down the road, and Sam had already visited and begun to get to know the teachers and the other children. The outside of the house had been newly decorated, and the front garden planted with shrubs, but the inside still needed some work.

Matt took the key from his pocket, handing it to Sam and lifting him up so that he could reach the lock.

'Is this *our* house now?'

Matt chuckled. 'Yes, it is. I've got something to show you when we get inside.'

'What?' Sam pushed the door open and Matt set him back on his feet. He rushed inside, looking around the sitting room and then running into the kitchen.

Hannah took Matt's arm, and they crossed the threshold of their new home. The sitting room had been painted, but the floorboards were bare and there was no furniture yet. The kitchen was old, but it would do until they could afford to replace it. The minute they'd seen the large, Victorian house, Matt and Hannah had known that this was the place where they wanted to raise a family and grow old together.

'Have the painters finished in Sam's room?' Hannah knew how much it meant to Matt to be a good father, and when she'd suggested he should be the one to decorate Sam's room, he'd jumped at the chance.

'You'll see.' Matt grinned at her, calling to Sam. 'Why don't you try upstairs?'

Sam clattered upstairs, running into the master bedroom, which was flooded with winter sunshine. Hannah followed him.

'Oh! Matt you bought a bed! It's beautiful…' It was the one she'd wanted, but had decided they couldn't afford. The snowy white quilt and pillows suited it perfectly.

'Have I got a bed too?' Sam asked.

'Go and see.' Matt was standing in the doorway, grinning.

Sam ran into the room he'd chosen as his bedroom. Hannah expected to hear some reaction, but there was a sudden silence. Matt caught her hand, and she followed him.

The room had been painted and the carpet laid. In one corner, a whole constellation of stars covered the ceiling, and models of each of the planets in the solar system were suspended on fine wires. There were bookshelves, some squashy beanbag seats, and a long low bench with a child's chair. On the other side of the room was a bunk bed with moon and stars bedding.

'Do you like it?' Matt seemed suddenly nervous, but when Sam turned around he was grinning from ear to ear.

'Can I sleep here? Tonight?'

'Oh, sweetie.' Hannah turned the corners of her mouth down. 'I want to sleep here too, but we can't. All our things are at home.'

'But I live *here* now.'

Matt chuckled. 'I packed a bag for us. We'll have to go back home tomorrow, Sam, the decorators will be working here again next week. But we can stay tonight and we'll bring the rest of your things here next weekend.'

'Yes! Thanks, Dad!'

Sam started to explore his room, and Hannah crooked her finger, indicating that they could leave him to it. Outside, in the hallway, Matt caught her in a sudden embrace, his eyes bright with emotion.

'I think I just got promoted.'

Sam had readily accepted that Matt was his dad now, but this was the first time he'd called him Dad.

'You've definitely earned it. I love you, Robin.'

He chuckled. 'And I love you, Flash.'

* * * * *

LET'S TALK

Romance

For exclusive extracts, competitions
and special offers, find us online:

f facebook.com/millsandboon

⊡ @millsandboonuk

🐦 @millsandboon

Or get in touch on 0844 844 1351*

For all the latest titles coming soon,
visit millsandboon.co.uk/nextmonth